WHITE DOVE, TELL ME

The Basque Series

White Dove, Tell Me

A Novel

MARTIN ETCHART

UNIVERSITY OF NEVADA PRESS | *Reno & Las Vegas*

University of Nevada Press | Reno, Nevada 89557 USA
www.unpress.nevada.edu
Copyright © 2024 by Martin Etchart
All rights reserved

Manufactured in the United States of America

FIRST PRINTING

Jacket design by TG Design
Jacket photograph © Sue McDonald/Shutterstock.com

Bible quotations are from the 1954 New Catholic Edition.

Library of Congress Cataloging-in-Publication Data on file
ISBN 978-1-64779-132-2 (cloth)
ISBN 978-1-64779-133-9 (ebook)
LCCN 2023942815

The paper used in this book meets the requirements of American National Standard for
Information Sciences—Permanence of Paper for Printed Library Materials, ANSI/NISO
Z39.48–1992 (R2002).

Urepel, Arizona, population 657, established 1927

PALM SUNDAY

No one knows the Son except the Father,
and no knows the Father except the Son.

MATTHEW 11:27

› › › *killing a pig*

The blood on the floor belongs to me, and my wife, Idetta, knows it.

"Damn it, Xabier, I told you to take your boots off outside." Idetta stands at the stove bouncing the crying baby on her hip and stirring a pot of lamb stew.

"I did." I drop my bloody socks into the sink and crank on the faucet; the pipes shudder before spitting out water. "Big pig—blood seeped through."

Idetta blows a dangling lock of hair out of her eyes. "Then why didn't you take off your socks?"

I wash pig's blood from my hands. "You didn't tell me to do that."

"And you couldn't figure it out?"

I give her a wink. "Too much thinking for a dumb Basque-O."

"Too little you mean." Idetta grabs a towel and thrusts the crying baby into my arms. "See what he wants."

As Idetta kneels to wipe up the blood, her yellow dress rides up her wide hips to expose thick calves. My wife is solid as a mare and moves through life like she's plowing a field. Only I won't tell her that. Unless I want a pop on the head. And even though we are both twenty-five, she seems older. Another thing best not to mention.

In an effort to quiet the baby, I sing to him, "Uso zuria, errazu."

It is the same song Aitatxi sings outside while he finishes butchering the pig. He's making tripota for next week's Easter meal. Something he hasn't done for years—not since Mom died. But Dad asked him to, and I'm glad because I've always liked blood sausage.

3

"Uso zuria, errazu, norat joaiten ziren zu?" I sing in Euskara and then repeat in English. "White dove tell me, where do you go?"

I don't know the rest of the song's words because Aitatxi only ever sings the beginning, over and over. I have no idea where the hell the white dove is going. So I sing, "To Paris? To France? To Spain?" Making up any place I want. "To Rome or Saturn or Mars?"

Today, my singing is definitely not what the baby wants. The sound of my voice makes him cry harder.

I scan the laminate countertop for the baby's pacifier and find it wedged between the chipped bowl my mother used to make Gâteau Basque and a new stainless steel Instant Pot.

My jaw muscles tighten.

Ever since the baby came, Idetta has been going on about how an Instant Pot would cut down her cooking time. I told her good food takes time. Idetta said a baby takes more. Then she went and bought the pot on credit without telling me.

As I snatch up the pacifier, my fingers graze the Instant Pot, but I don't say anything. In the year we've been married, I've learned that Basque women in general, and Idetta in particular, shouldn't be argued with while cleaning up after a Basque man.

I try to slip the pacifier into the baby's mouth. But it's a no-go; he spits it out. Sobs rack his two-month-old body. His tiny hands curl into tiny fists. He wails.

I think not having an official name is the reason he's upset—a primal need for identity causing his distress. I want to name my son Ferdinand, after my father. But since the boy was born in Arizona and not Euskal Herria, Idetta thinks it's too ethnic and wants a more American name.

Justin is high on her list.

"Ferdinand," I whisper into my son's ear.

Idetta glares up at me. "That's not his name."

Even though we need to agree on a name soon—the baptism

4

is scheduled for the week after Easter—I don't push it. Instead, I remind myself I'm lucky Idetta married me. Every so often I forget she said, *I do,* and imagine her saying, *I don't.* If I told Idetta this, she would frown and ask me why I would think such a thing. And what could I say? Sometimes I find the past difficult to accept and the present hard to remember.

I hum and rock the baby from side to side.

Idetta gets to her feet. With her back to me, she throws the bloody towel into the sink and turns on the water. As her dark hair falls over one bare shoulder, like a rope knotted to the base of my spine, longing draws me to her.

I slide in behind Idetta and press against her body.

"Really? Now, Xabier?"

As she washes out the bloody towel, I take her left ear lobe between my lips and hold the tiny wooden flower I carved in front of her face.

"You could have picked me a real flower."

I nibble her neck. "Real flowers die, but like our love, this will last forever."

Idetta drapes the towel over the faucet. "Did you use the pig knife to carve it?"

"I cleaned off the blood first."

"Ugh." She elbows me in the ribs and takes the crying baby. "Call your father and Aitatxi in for lunch."

Before I turn away, Idetta plucks the tiny flower from my hand and places it on the windowsill alongside all my other wooden carvings.

"A little blood never hurt anything," she says with a hint of a smile—then coos to the baby, "Isn't that right, Justin."

"Oh hell no." I yank open the door. "You are not going to name my son after some tatted-up pop singer. I'll carve Ferdinand on his ass before I let that happen."

I shut the door behind me with a bang. Inside, Idetta laughs. I laugh too—dumb Basque-O. I step over the sleeping sheepdogs,

Txauri and Haugi, and to avoid splinters, tiptoe to the edge of the porch. There, I shade my eyes against the sharp April sun.

Sheep move in a rippling wave of white through the west pasture. Beyond the flock, at the edge of our 640-acre ranch, a patch of brown desert butts up against the Colorado River—the spot where Aitatxi and Amatxi built their original homestead. From where I stand, the river's water is hidden from view as it rushes through a deep cut in the earth.

On the horizon, there's a cluster of dark clouds—a harbinger of a thunderstorm. But the storm is still a ways off. I will have time to cover the hay bales and put the horses in the barn and take down the pig hanging from the hook fastened to the barn's sloping western wall.

The pig's front legs dangle above the dented bucket Aitatxi catches blood in—like the animal is trying to dive into the bucket as the last of its life drains away. Aitatxi pours the blood into a cast-iron pot. Then he sets the pot atop a grill; flames flicker up between the grates.

I call to Aitatxi across the open area where chickens peck the dirt. "Where's Dad?"

Aitatxi waves toward the barn.

Dad's been working on our old Farmall tractor since we got home from Mass. Last month, he replaced the clutch—the month before, the carburetor. He is determined to get one more season out of the Farmall. My father can be hardheaded. Something Idetta likes to point out I inherited.

I yell from the porch, waking the dogs who start to bark. "Lunch!"

In response, my father lets out his irrintzina, "Ai-ai-ai-ai-ai-ai-ai-yaaaaa!" The cry my Basque ancestors used to call to each other across the Pyrenees.

The chickens cluck and the dogs bark and the sheep baaa and Aitatxi sings, "Uso zuria, errazu," and metal tears and wood snaps and Dad's irrintzina turns to a scream.

6

Dust billows out the barn's open doorway as Aitatxi drops his bloody bucket—Txauri and Haugi leap from the porch—I run with sharp gravel biting my feet.

At the barn's entrance, dust hangs in a curtain in front of me—obscuring the broken rafter beam, the red Farmall with its missing tire, the come-along winch and chain lying in a heap on the ground.

Txauri and Haugi bark and bark and bark.

"Dad?" I step farther into the barn—the dust clears—and Aitatxi wails as he falls to his knees at the blood on the floor.

SPY WEDNESDAY

Blessed are they that mourn:
for they shall be comforted.

MATTHEW 5:4

› › › *planning a funeral*

On the day of my father's funeral, I don't know if my hands should go up and over or under and across. As I grasp the tie in my fingers, the black material spills down the front of my white shirt. I need to give form to the thing I hold, but I can't remember how.

Dad taught me to knot a tie when I was twelve years old, standing behind me, calloused hands encompassing mine.

"Don't worry if you get it right, Xabier." My father guided my movement. "You can always start over."

Today there can be no starting over.

My pale face fills the bedroom mirror. The shapeless black tie remains draped around my neck. A thickness clouds my thoughts like I am waking from a too-long nap, disoriented and waiting for the world to settle back into focus. I see and un-see my father's hand reaching from beneath the Farmall.

"Oh, my Xabier." Idetta carries the sleeping baby into the room. "We're going to be late."

"I can't believe he's gone."

"I know, my love." Idetta lays the baby on the bed. Then she steps between me and the mirror and takes hold of my tie.

I drop my arms to my sides and stand there like a boy—helpless and not knowing how to do the things asked of me. "I don't understand."

"Maybe there is no understanding." Idetta moves the tie under and across and then flips it up and over. "Only acceptance."

I nod dumbly.

Idetta presses her warm palm against my cheek. "We need to hurry—I set out a tray for Aitatxi."

Idetta disappears into the bathroom. I pick up the sleeping baby and can barely feel the weight of him as he settles into the crook of my arm—like it is the safest place in the world.

But is any place safe after what happened to my father?

A tremble ripples through me. I place a protective hand on my son's head and carry him from the room.

After I retrieve the tray from the kitchen, I take it and the baby up the creaking wooden stairs to Aitatxi's bedroom.

The room is cool and dark. The breakfast tray of sourdough toast and fried eggs sits untouched on the nightstand. Aitatxi has hardly eaten since the accident. Four days now, lying in bed with his eyes closed, mumbling in Euskara, "Maitea gatik pasa nintza-ske gauak eta egunak." As if he has forgotten the English of his adopted country—a language it took him years to learn.

When I was a baby, Aitatxi would practice his English by carrying me around the ranch and pointing out things: "This a sheep; she for wool. That a cactus; it of thorns. Those coyotes; they need watching." As a teenager, I mentioned to Aitatxi how I recalled him doing that. He said it was impossible, I was just a baby. But Aitatxi was wrong. I remembered his words and the firmness of his muscles and the roughness of his stubble and the bitter-sweet odor of his skin.

This Aitatxi; he forever.

I set the lunch tray down and press the back of my hand to his forehead; his skin is as dry as stone. What is he thinking—dreaming? Of Dad when he was a boy? Of the green mountains of Euskal Herria? Or is his head, like mine, full of the *what ifs* of my father's last day?

What if before tracking blood into the kitchen, I went into the barn to check on my father?

What if when I saw the chain draped over the wooden beam and the come-along winch attached to the front of the Farmall, I said the words he used so often on me, "You think that's a smart thing to do?"

What if I pointed out to my father the weakness in the wood—the way the beam splintered and bowed?

What if I told him we should go to Mendia's Feed and Tackle and buy a tractor jack?

What if he agreed?

What if he and I and Aitatxi and Idetta and the baby had been sitting together eating lunch when the beam snapped under the weight of the tractor?

What if after we all went into the barn and shook our heads with relief over what could have happened but didn't?

And there would have been no blood on the floor and no hand reaching out from under the tractor and Dad would still be here.

What if?

At the foot of Aitatxi's bed lies the bunched-up quilt Mom and Amatxi made the summer I turned ten. A tangle of red and yellow roses is sewn into the material. The roses hold the faded memory of a garden—flowers and vegetables planted over by the corral. The garden plowed under years ago.

Careful not to wake the baby, I pull the quilt up over Aitatxi. "You gotta eat something, Aitatxi."

For answer, he mutters, "Gauak eta egunak, desertu eta oihanak."

I frown. I never really learned the Basque language. Oh, I picked up some words and phrases, a few lyrics from the songs Aitatxi sang while working and greetings to friends: "Nola zira?"—How are you? And, of course, commands to the sheep dogs, who apparently spoke Euskara too: "etorri"—come; "joan"—go. But my father never wanted me to learn Euskara; he said it was a "dead language."

Only growing up on the ranch, Euskara appeared to be very much alive. Dad and Aitatxi spoke it while tending sheep, "Zazte ardian bila." Mom murmured it to Dad as they sat on the porch, "Nola zen zuri egun?" And every night, Amatxi came into my room and whispered, "Ondo ibili ene maitasuna."

I knew what some of Amatxi's words meant—"ondo," good, "ene," mine, "maite," love—but I didn't understand how the words went together to form meaning. And I never asked for it to be explained because that would have ruined the magic of the secret message Amatxi sent me off to buba with each night.

Looking back, I now see the distance my not speaking Euskara created between my family and me. A chasm needing a bridge to cross. A bridge my father chose not to help me build.

Aitatxi mumbles, "Usoa eder airean."

Has Aitatxi forgotten where he is? Traveled back to Euskal Herria? Will he ever return?

Dr. Berria told me there is nothing physically wrong with Aitatxi. He just suffers from grief. And grief can't kill a person, right?

"Come back, Aitatxi." I manage a weak chuckle that brings tears to my eyes. "Who's going to make the tripota?"

But Aitatxi gives no indication he hears me.

I pull open the curtains and let sunlight fall into the room. Through the window, I look down at the closed barn doors. There, the sheep dogs, Haugi and Txauri, huddle in the dirt as if waiting for Dad to appear and tell them what to do.

The hook for the pig still hangs from the side of the barn. But the pig is gone. As well as the blood. My friends, Louie and Jean, cleaning up.

Beyond the barn, where the flock wanders like a drifting cloud over the land, everything seems so quiet and peaceful and the same as always—only it isn't the same, and never will be again.

I wanted to wait to have my father's funeral. Another week—longer. But Idetta told me we couldn't.

"If we don't do it now, we'll have to wait until after Easter."

I sat on the edge of our bed, folding and unfolding my hands; my thick fingers fumble over each other as if trying to put back together a piece of equipment broken beyond repair. I wanted to say to her, *For Christ sake can't we put it off until the world quits shaking under me?* And explain how I lost my balance with every step I took and had to catch myself to keep from falling. I wanted to press her palm flat against my stomach and let her feel the quivering inside me—how I was no longer solid.

"The spring lambs are coming." Idetta put the baby in his crib. "And then there's the baptism. We need to be ready, Xabier."

I balled up my hands so that my fingernails cut into the skin of my palms. "I'm not ready."

"Ready or not, the future will come," Idetta said.

I couldn't stop my father's funeral. No more than I could stop my mother getting cancer and dissolving in front of my eyes when I was twelve, or Amatxi lying down for a nap and never getting up the day after I turned sixteen.

My hands fell open. "I'll call the apaiza."

I turn from Aitatxi's window as the baby wakes and starts to cry.

At the sound of the baby's sobs, Aitatxi mumbles, "Maitea gatik pasa nintzazke gauak eta egunak."

His words intertwine with the baby's crying as though the two of them are speaking a language only they understand.

› › › finding a dove

The church's gravel parking lot is full.

All of Urepel turning out for one of their own.

Like always, common Basque heritage draws us together. The town was founded by a handful of immigrants who crossed the warm waters of the Colorado River into Arizona. One Basque family followed after another. Until, like flotsam gathering in an eddy, they banded together. Then, keeping with the long Basque tradition of unoriginal but accurate place-naming, called their new home Urepel—"warm water."

Dust rises around the people I have known my entire life as they greet each other with handshakes and hugs. The scene is familiar and oddly comforting—like a traditional Basque picnic where everyone takes time off from work to celebrate as a community.

But that illusion is destroyed by the black suits and dresses filing into the church.

I should be grateful for the friends who have gathered to honor my father. But instead a cold knot settles in my chest. They shouldn't be here. *We shouldn't be here.* I shake my head. Dad would have hated his funeral. Public attention embarrassed him.

My father, Ferdinand Etxea, was a quiet man, shy and private, who worked hard and loved his family.

I have rehearsed these words in my head and plan to say them when asked. True words, simple and to the point—like him. Words I will use to keep from having to explain how my father's death feels different from my mother's or Amatxi's—as if a chunk of myself has been cut away.

Is it because I'm older? Have spent more years with my father? Did all that extra time embed him more deeply in my flesh?

Dad *there* for all twenty-five years of my life but now *gone* for the last four days.

My rehearsed words seem foolish and inadequate. The privacy my father wrapped himself in has been torn away—because there is nothing private about death.

I pull my truck into the parking lot's last empty space between Jean Etxeberri's white Dodge and the red Ford Louie Mendia inherited from his father. The Ford's dented back bumper is a reminder of how at fifteen, Louie, Jean, and I got a six-pack and took the truck out for a midnight drive and ended up backing into a water pump. Only we didn't tell Louie's father that. Instead, we threw away the empty beer cans, washed off the truck, and parked it where we'd found it. Later, Louie's father couldn't understand how the dent got there. When asked, the three of us shrugged in feigned ignorance.

Louie's twin boys, Carl and Max, race by my window. I shake my head; it's just a matter of time before that Ford gets another dent.

A few cars over, Mari Ainciart braids her dark hair while talking with Arlete Bastanchury; the two girls break into giggles. The widowed Irigoyen sisters share a frown as arm in arm they stride past.

"Don't you ever clean this thing?" Idetta brushes flakes of alfalfa off the front of her dress. She asks me the same question every time she rides in my truck.

I turn off the ignition. "I'll get the baby."

When I open the truck's back door, I find my son sleeping with a rubber toy sheep wedged in his mouth.

What are you dreaming? Is Dad in your dreams? Like he is in mine?

Each night since my father's death, I have heard his voice in my sleep. His final scream from the barn winds its way through my body and squeezes tight my chest. I wake gasping. A word hidden within his primal scream? If so, I cannot make it out. His voice too distant, too distorted to be clear. Until last night when Dad's scream changed to a whisper, his lips brushing against my ear as the word took shape—"arima."

I sat straight up in bed, leaning into the darkness, my hand rising to where the memory of his touch lingered.

"Arima"—the last word Mom said to Dad the day she died.

"Ferdinand, don't lose your arima," she told him.

"Noeline," my father responded, "you are my arima."

I'd never heard the word before. "Arima." At my mother's funeral, I rolled the word inside my mouth, the letters round and soft and secret. "Arima." I swallowed the word as the apaiza threw a handful of dirt on her coffin, "For dust you are and to dust shall you return." "Arima." The word lodged like an ember in my chest. "Arima." Mom had told Dad not to lose his arima, and I vowed not to lose mine either.

Then realizing I didn't know what I planned on not losing, I decided to ask Amatxi the meaning of the word.

I found her in the kitchen making sourdough.

Whenever Amatxi got in an argument with Aitatxi or I got in trouble at school or there was a funeral, Amatxi baked: meringues, pecan turnovers, French chocolate rolls, Gateau Basque, and lots of sourdough bread.

She was flouring the countertop as I walked in and parked myself in a chair.

"It no time for dinner." Amatxi slapped the sourdough down and began working it.

"I know."

"Then why you need?"

I kicked at a loose plank in the wood floor. "What's arima?"

Amatxi stopped working the dough and pinched her lips together, seemingly unsure of the answer. Then she gazed out the kitchen window as if the word's meaning lay somewhere beyond the glass. "It mean hope. Now go, I have bread a bake."

"Arima." I feel the word on my lips as I unhook the baby's car seat from the base and lift him out. On this horrible day, I am lucky to have him as my arima.

Idetta walks around the front of the truck and takes my free hand. "Just breathe, Xabier."

As we move toward the church, I keep my head down, afraid the grief in the faces of my friends will overwhelm me.

When we reach the front steps, Idetta stops. "I forgot the diaper bag."

I hand her the baby and head back toward the truck.

By the time I retrieve the diaper bag from under the passenger seat, the parking lot is empty. Everyone inside the church.

I linger where I am, with my hand on top of the truck's open door.

I don't have to go in.

Overhead, the sun burns the sky white.

I can just stay here.

Sweat gathers on my collar.

Where there are no mourners, no coffin, no death. Just me and the sun and rows of empty cars.

But there is no escape. Eventually, Idetta will come out, frowning and angry with me for being late for my own father's funeral—making this bad day even worse.

I hitch the diaper bag over my right shoulder and swing shut the door to reveal a white dove sitting on the gravel in front of my truck. The bird's feathers glow like the unblemished wool of a newborn lamb.

The dove begins to coo, a deep, throaty pulsing.

The bird doesn't belong here. The dove's whiteness foreign to the desert. It must have been released at some kind of celebration—a wedding, birthday, or funeral.

Loose gravel pops under tires.

A red car pulls into the parking lot. A late arriver. The car is going a little too fast as it heads straight toward me and the dove. The stupid bird will be run over. And because right here, right now, I can't handle any more death, I take a step forward and raise my arms to shoo the bird away. But the dove doesn't move.

"Go!" I stomp my foot. "Get out of here!"

The white dove takes flight, rises into the sun, and vanishes.

I blink away the black spots and scan the surrounding sky, but the dove has disappeared.

The honking of a horn pulls my attention down as the car comes to a skidding stop with the bumper only inches from me.

Sunlight reflects off the windshield so I can't make out the driver.

Then a cloud moves in front of the sun, darkening the windshield, and I fix my eyes on my ex-fiancée, Jenny Pernice.

I mouth the words, *What the fuck?*

Jenny waves a trickle of fingers at me as the church bells begin to ring.

Shit—I stuff the diaper bag under my arm and race to my father's funeral.

› › › *making a prayer*

My knees ache from kneeling as the apaiza, Father Kieran, quotes Saint Ignatius. "For it is not knowing much, but realizing and relishing things interiorly, that contents and satisfies the soul."

My father's closed casket sits in front of the altar; if I stretch out my hand, my fingers could graze the smooth, dark wood.

Dad? Are you really in there?

I tighten my fingers on the pew's wooden handrail carved by Aitatxi. When I was a boy, Aitatxi taught me about the different chisels, and how each one had a special purpose and left a unique mark. Across the aisle, the Basque cross lauburus Aitatxi carved into the ends of each row are frozen pinwheels in time.

"Like Mother Teresa preached"—Father Kieran grips the pulpit—"not all of us can do great things. But we can do small things with great love."

Father Kieran's habit of stringing quotes together annoyed my father. He said the apaiza did it because he was too young to have any thoughts of his own. And the apaiza is young—younger than me. He's also Irish and not an Esqualuna—of Basque descent—and has been in Urepel for only three months.

When he preaches, Father Kieran's leg bounces with nervous excitement, like a boy asking a girl out on a first date. Which he may or may not have ever done.

Why am I thinking about that?

The incense from the altar irritates my nose. I try not to sneeze like I did at my wedding when Idetta and I stood on the exact spot where the casket now sits. I sneezed ten times in a row before I managed, "I do." Thankfully, everyone—including Idetta—laughed.

"As Saint Francis tell us," Father Kieran says, "we shall steer safely through every storm, so long as our heart is right, our intention fervent, our courage steadfast, and our trust fixed on God."

Usually, Father Kieran's quotes don't bother me. Sometimes they're even funny, like when he drops in lines from movies ("Like Clint Eastwood said, Jesus is asking you to, 'Make my day' by being holy.") During Palm Sunday's Mass, when the apaiza used a quote from Tarantino's latest film, Dad's scowl cut rows of a fallow field into his forehead.

"Saint Paul tells us in Corinthians that your life is not your own; it has been bought with a price." Father Kieran raises a finger for emphasis. "And the only way to buy it back is with the currency of love."

Dad's life not his own? Huh? Currency of love?

I have the uncharitable desire to punch the apaiza in the throat.

My father would not be happy with Father Kieran presiding over his funeral. He liked our old apaiza, Father Mathieu, who *was* an Esqualuna from Biarritz, France. Father Mathieu was at our parish for forty-two years, before he retired and moved to Newport Beach, California. At his last homily, Father Mathieu said, "Though I've grown to love the desert, my heart belongs to the sea."

I notice a familiar rhythm to Father Kieran's words... something about "the news today"...holy shit, it's U2. Father Kieran is quoting lyrics from "Sunday Bloody Sunday" at my dad's funeral!

I clasp my hands together as if I'm praying, but I'm not. I can't pray. Prayer requires thinking and I can't think—not clearly—not with everything so jumbled up inside. The lambs are coming while Aitatxi sings in Euskara and the apaiza quotes Bono and Idetta wipes up the blood on the floor with Jenny gazing at me through the sun-splattered windshield of her car.

What the hell is she even doing at my father's funeral? Didn't she move to Los Angeles?

At least, that's what she told me in her last text—the one she used to break up with me. *I need more.* More what? More land? More sky?

Stop thinking of Jenny.

My father is dead. I need to think of him.

Only Dad doesn't feel dead.

I never saw his body. Just the one hand. It could have been anybody's hand. Reaching? Grasping? For what?

Idetta went to the morgue to identify the remains. Not me.

What if she got it wrong?

I shut my eyes...when I get back to the ranch, the sun will shine. The baaing of sheep will float through the air. Dad will be there, standing amid the flock, pushing back his cap and smelling of dust and sheep and sweat. The dryness of the land on my tongue; the solid earth beneath my feet. My father will ask how Mass went. I will smile and tell him, "Too many quotes and not enough music." And Dad will laugh and I will laugh and the world will be as it was.

Idetta elbows me in the side and whispers fiercely, "Quit smiling."

Dumb Basque-O—Dad is gone—it can't be imagined away. With my eyes still shut, I squeeze my entwined fingers and force out a prayer—*Please God, just let this be over.*

The church goes silent.

I open my eyes to find Father Kieran has come down from the altar to stand in front of my father's casket. The apaiza twists the fingers of his hands together, seemingly unsure of which quote in his arsenal to whip out next. Saint Francis? Pope John Paul? Justin Bieber?

Finally, Father Kieran says, "I didn't know Ferdinand Etxea. Not the way you did—the way you still do. But I know this, Easter is nearing and just as Jesus will again rise from the dead, Ferdinand too will rise and come to each of you in his own way to let you know he is all right. So be vigilant and in the words of Saint Mark, 'What I say to you, I say to all: Watch!' Now let us pray."

When everyone around me gets to their feet to join the apaiza in prayer, I remain on my knees, hands still clasped together, as if holding onto my father, anchoring him to this earth for a moment longer, knowing when I rise he too will rise and float off to a heaven that right now I wish didn't exist.

I lift my eyes to the life-size crucifix behind the altar. Jesus's downcast gaze is fixed on my father's casket as the light from the altar's candles reflects off polished wood, flickering and jumping and spreading out like the wings of a dove.

I suck in my breath.

Be vigilant. Watch.

The white dove in the parking lot. The words to the song Aitatxi sang the day of the accident, "Uso zuria errazu...white dove tell me..."

Dad? The white dove? There for me?

And me sending the dove away because I hadn't known what to be vigilant for. Or how to watch.

When Father Kieran turns back to the altar, Idetta pulls me to my feet for communion.

› › › *drinking a beer*

I feel lost in my own home.

Like an overexposed photo, everything too bright. The world made up of sharp edges and jutting angles with no shadows to hide in.

Hands reach out and clasp my arm, followed by the same words over and over: "Xabier, I'm so sorry."

People fill the house Aitatxi built. They sit in the chairs we made together. They lean on the mantel I helped carve.

"Each piece a wood, it have isiliko behotza—secret heart," Aitatxi told me when I was a boy and he still talked about one day opening a furniture store. But then the flock just kept growing and there was no time for carving—only sheep.

Voices rise and fall—some in Euskara, others in English as the two languages mix and swirl and collide. I can't seem to catch a good breath because even though I grew up here and have lived my whole life inside these walls and am familiar with every corner and turn, today this place is foreign to me, changed by the absence of my father.

Fred Big grabs my arm and pulls me into a corner.

Fred used to be a cattle rancher, but he lost everything during the recession of 2008. Now he's the only sheriff in Urepel—and banker and realtor and insurance agent.

In a breath sour with red wine, he whispers, "Don't worry, Xabier, there won't be no investigation."

I have no idea what he's talking about.

With a wink, Fred slaps me on the back and goes to refill his wine glass.

I push my way through the crowded living room and stumble

into the kitchen where bottles of wine and loaves of sourdough bread crowd the countertop. Red grenadine stains my mother's white tablecloth as the ancient Irigoyen sisters argue over the proper way to make a Picon cocktail.

Henriette Irigoyen grabs the bottle of Amer Picon from her sister. "You put in too much."

Isabelle Irigoyen snatches the bottle back. "I don't like it sweet."

As their gnarled hands wring the bottle's neck, Henriette notices me out of the corner of her eye. "Isilik."

Isabelle turns toward me. With their hands still clutching the bottle, the sisters glare at me as if I am a twelve-year-old intruding on an adult conversation. I duck my head and bolt out the back door. On the porch, I collapse over the railing and take long, slow pulls of air.

Damn day—end already.

A rooster crows, the sheep baaa, Haugi and Txauri bark. The familiar sounds of the ranch loosen the tightness in my chest. Some things haven't changed. I straighten up and push my fingers through my sweat-matted hair. As I undo the tie around my neck, I can't help but scan the area for a glimpse of white—the flutter of wings. But the only white I find belongs to the sheep in the pasture; the only birds I see are chickens.

I kick the porch's nearest wood post.

What did I expect? Dad to come swooping down from heaven? To push open the doors of the barn and step into the sunlight?

Louie stumbles out onto the porch—almost dropping the two bottles of beer he holds. "Shit those Irigoyen sisters still scare the hell out of me."

"Tell me about it."

Louie sips foam off the top of one beer and hands me the other. "Remember the time the sisters caught us stealing apples from their tree?"

"They caught you." I take a sip. "And you threw me under the bus."

Louie clinks his bottle against mine. "What are friends for?"

I let out a dry chuckle that turns into a cough. The host from Communion feels stuck in my throat.

For a moment, Louie and I just stand there, drinking and looking out over the ranch.

"How's your aitatxi doing?" Louie asks as he leans against a post.

"Same."

"You know, I once saw him use his bare hands to rip a piece of sheet metal in half like it was paper."

I smile. "Just last week, he walked across the pasture with a pregnant ewe tucked under each of his arms."

Louie shakes his head. "God don't make tough like that no more."

And I wonder if that's true. Because the aitatxi who lies mumbling in bed upstairs seems old and fragile—as if all the toughness has been ripped out of him—leaving behind only a discarded husk.

Louie clears his throat. "You know, I can help you out with the lambing."

"You've got the store to take care of." I peel the label from the beer bottle and roll the moist paper between my fingers. "I'll manage."

"How?"

"No fucking idea."

Louie laughs and throws an arm around my shoulder. I laugh too—and for the first time in this whole shitty day life feels normal.

But then the laughter fades. Louie pulls his arm away. And we go back to sipping our beers in silence as awkwardness again settles over us.

On the far side of the pasture, a dust devil kicks to life. The funnel of dirt rises, twisting and turning, darkening and swelling as it struggles to break free from the earth—to reach the clouds that have forever floated out of reach. The dust devil climbs higher—tail lifting from the ground. *Now is my time—I will not fail.* But the heart of the dust devil gives out as its body grows translucent, dissipates, and falls in particles back to the ground—for *dust you are and to dust shall you return.*

Louie bumps my shoulder. "Why was Jenny at the church?"

"How the hell should I know?"

"You didn't hear she was back?"

"No." I eye Louie suspiciously. "Did you?"

"I might have heard something about her staying in Kingman."

"Thanks for the heads-up."

"I didn't think you'd want to know."

"I don't." I toss my empty beer bottle into the yard, scattering the chickens. "I thought she still lived in Los Angeles."

"I heard she ran out of money."

"You sure hear a lot."

Louie winds up like a pitcher and sends his bottle flying. "What can I say, my wife's got lots of friends."

"What the hell was Jenny thinking, coming to my father's funeral?"

"Maybe she liked your dad."

"She didn't even know my dad."

Louie winks. "Maybe she's got a thing for funerals."

In spite of myself, I chuckle. "You're sick."

"Now you sound like my wife."

From inside the house come the sounds of something crashing. "Carl! Max!" Louie's wife, Pascaline, yells. "Louie!"

"That's my cue." Louie slaps me on the back. "Coming dear!"

As Louie hustles inside, someone drives up the dirt road. The chickens rush to keep from getting squashed. I recognize the red car from the church parking lot—*You gotta be fucking kidding me.*

My face flushes with heat as I glance over my shoulder, half expecting Idetta to be standing there. I have never discussed what happened between Jenny and me with my wife. Not the specifics anyway. But Idetta is one of Pascaline's best friends. So I'm sure she's heard plenty.

Since I don't need any more drama—not today—I jump off the porch to intercept Jenny. When she tries to get out of her car, I slap my hand against the driver's door and keep it closed.

Jenny rolls down her window. "Hey Xabier."

I wipe away the spittle gathered at the corners of my mouth. "Get out of here before my wife comes out."

Jenny tucks her blonde hair behind her ears—a move I remember well. "I'd love to meet her."

"Not going to happen."

Jenny smiles. "Still holding on to the past I see."

"Nope." I fold my arms across my chest. "In fact, as far as I'm concerned, you never existed."

That takes the smile off Jenny's face. Her eyes go moist. And suddenly, it's like all the time she's been gone never happened and she is still the girl I grew up with, told my secrets to, shared my first kiss with, and gave Mom's wedding ring the day I asked her to marry me. Only she's not. She's the girl who promised to love me forever, then ran off in the middle of the night, sent me a text for explanation, and broke my heart.

Even though I shouldn't care—even though I don't care—my chest tightens and all the feelings I'd scraped away and discarded come rushing back, and I again feel like I'm the one who has done something wrong and longs for a chance to make it right.

With a flick of her hair, Jenny regains her composure. "You're such an ass, Xabier."

"I haven't spoken to you in two years and you show up at my father's funeral, and I'm an ass?"

Jenny lets out an exaggerated sigh. "That's why I'm here—to talk about your father."

"What kind of crazy are you?"

Jenny gives me one of her patented eye rolls. "I'm serious, Xabier. It's important."

"You didn't even know my father."

"Actually, Ferdinand and I had been meeting up once a week for the last three months."

Jenny's words slug into me; I kick the side of her car. "What the hell is wrong with you?"

"You need to understand—"

—I punch her side mirror, shattering the glass and bloodying my knuckles.

"Stop it, Xabier."

"You show up here and say shit like that right after my dad died?"

"It's about how he died, I—"

—I grab a rock to smash her windshield.

Jenny slams her car into gear and fishtails away. I heave the rock after her as she flips me the bird and speeds off.

The back porch door bangs open. I spin around anticipating Idetta and instead find Louie holding two beers and shaking his head.

› › › *talking to Aitatxi*

My bloodied knuckles are wrapped in a dish towel as I spoon vermicelli soup into Aitatxi's mouth.

Luckily, no one but Louie saw what took place. I told Idetta I banged my knuckles on the porch railing. I'm not sure she believed me, but she pressed the palm of her hand to my cheek and said, "Oh, my Xabier."

Aitatxi's eyes remain closed as I feed him—most of the soup seeping out the corners of his mouth.

From where I sit, the top of the barn's pitched roof is visible. I haven't been in the barn since the accident and don't know what waits for me. Dried blood on the floor? The come-along winch draped over a sawhorse? The broken Farmall listing on its side?

"Jenny was here," I tell Aitatxi as I wipe away the liquid with the edge of a napkin. "You remember her—that bitch who screwed me over."

Aitatxi doesn't like when I swear and once told me there were no txarra words in Euskara. Which I immediately doubted since I'd heard both him and my father uttering phrases when they dropped a bale of hay on their foot or caught a finger in a closing gate that I am sure had nothing to do with *what a beautiful day it was.*

"Bitch, bitch, bitch." I lean forward and search Aitatxi's face for a reaction—a furrowing of his brow, a downturn of his mouth. But his face remains blank, as if my words hold no weight.

"She said she'd been meeting up with Dad." I plunk the bowl of soup onto the nightstand. "She said I needed to understand something about how Dad died. What the hell is there to understand? He was crushed by a tractor."

If Aitatxi were totally here, I probably wouldn't be telling him anything about Jenny. The stuff we talked about mostly revolved around either sheep—raising, feeding, castrating, shearing, and selling—or the past, like how Aitatxi met Amatxi at a Basque picnic in Chino, California, despite having grown up with her in Les Aldudes—a tiny village high in the Pyrenees. When I asked Aitatxi why he traveled over five thousand miles to meet the girl next door, he said, "I waiting for right time."

My phone dings. Jenny's name appears along with a text: *There are things you don't know.* I delete her text. Another follows: *We need to talk.*

I should have changed my number. Or erased her contact. Only I didn't.

Before I can press delete, a third text appears: *It's about his arima.*

His hope? Shit, how does Jenny even know that word? Did I tell it to her back when we shared our secrets? Or at least I shared mine. Jenny kept her secrets to herself.

I turn off my phone.

A clatter of dishes comes from downstairs. The house mostly empty now. Family and friends having returned to their unbroken lives and leaving me here to piece mine back together.

Pascaline stayed behind to help Idetta clean up. Their voices rise through the floorboards, but I can't make out what they're saying. How much did Louie tell his wife about Jenny? How much is she telling my wife? Did Louie tell Pascaline how Jenny and I met in biology class my sophomore year at U of A? How she used to ride on my lap while I plowed the fields? How we talked about getting married on the ranch? How she dumped me to go to LA and then showed up at my father's funeral?

"The thing is, Aitatxi, Jenny did look good." I lean back in my chair. "I mean, her hair is longer and—why the hell couldn't she just have gotten fat or something?"

Aitatxi draws in a gasping breath of air. When he exhales, the air comes out like barbed wire grating over stone.

I put a hand on his chest and whisper, "This Aitatxi; he forever."

Dusk creeps through the window to blanket the room in orange.

In the changing light, the gray bedposts stretch like reaching arms toward the ceiling; Amatxi's white dresser shines as if lit from inside; the ironwood table in the corner retreats into invisibility, leaving the items on it floating in midair—Aitatxi and Amatxi's wedding picture, his pocket knife and black beret, a bottle of Brut aftershave.

Where is the rest of your life, Aitatxi? Hidden in a closet? Crammed into a chest?

The air deepens from orange to red. Aitatxi's features blur in the failing light, making him unrecognizable as my aitatxi.

He is just an old man, in a bed, struggling for breath.

Is the end of forever here?

I move to the window to shut the curtains. Slits of light seep through gaps in the barn's walls.

Someone must have been in there earlier and left a light on.

Bitterness sours the back of my tongue.

Has the place of my father's death become an exhibition?

Then I spot the dove, a flicker of white rising into the darkening sky; the dove lands on the crest of the barn's roof as the last rays of the setting sun shoot from the horizon to race over the land and strike the dove—igniting it like a beacon of white-hot arima.

› › › *searching the night*

I wait until Idetta goes to put the baby to bed to grab a flashlight and head to the barn.

If I let Idetta know that on the day of his funeral I am going to the spot where my father died, she will frown, put her right hand on her hip, and ask, "Why, Xabier?"

What could I say? That I saw a white dove atop the barn and it turned into a flame of light? Or that I think the dove might be a sign from Dad—hell, maybe even be him?

No thank you.

Also, if I did tell Idetta about the white dove, then I'd have to tell her about the church parking lot where I first saw the dove, which would run me smack into Jenny.

Double no thank you.

Okay, so maybe my sneaking out of the house has more to do with me worrying about myself than my wife. But hell, how am I supposed to explain to her something I don't understand? How, even though I dropped a handful of dirt onto his coffin at the cemetery, my father being gone doesn't feel real to me?

It's crazy and stupid and maybe I am a dumb Basque-O—but I don't care. Because right now there's a tractor plowing through my head so that nothing makes sense in this crazy-stupid-dumb world.

The barn is dark.

Did the bulb burn out? Or did someone turn off the light? Idetta? Pascaline?

I click on my flashlight, walk across the open area, and run the beam over the barn's roof—nothing. I pour light over the barn's doors, illuminating peeling paint and rusted handles.

I intended to enter the barn. Only now I can't make myself do it. The fear of what I won't find inside stops me.

No white dove.

No Dad.

But since right now I am unwilling to have the fever dream of my father end, I move around to the side of barn. There, bales of broken straw litter the ground. On the wall, the hook for the pig still hangs. Next to it is the grill surrounded by discarded tractor parts embedded in the dirt.

I weave my way through them toward the back of the barn. When I round the corner, I come to an abrupt stop—a dark figure huddles there.

Dad?

My shaking flashlight beam plays over the figure. Blank. Faceless. A tarp thrown over a piece of old equipment.

I collapse forward. Hands on knees. Breaths quick and sharp.

What am I doing to myself? There is nothing here. Nothing hidden to find.

I step forward, grab the edge of the tarp, and yank it off. The tarp catches and tears like the shedding skin of a rattlesnake before revealing my old motorbike.

Two flat tires. Busted handlebars. Missing seat.

As I stand with the tarp clutched in my hand, the motorbike revs to life and carries me back to the day after I turned sixteen and Amatxi died.

I'd woken early, excited to drive my birthday present over to show Louie.

Unfortunately for me, Amatxi woke earlier. As I exited my room, she blocked the hallway like a stone lodged in the earth— tiny and sturdy and immovable.

"You clean up you mess before go."

"You're kidding, right?"

"No kid." Amatxi set her hands on her hips.

"I'm sixteen now."

Amatxi pointed toward my bedroom. "Baina, you old enough a clean you mess."

"I'll do it later."

Amatxi pulled the motorbike key from her pocket. "You do orai or you go take walk."

I banged my hand against the wall. "Sometimes I hate you, Amatxi."

"Sometime, I no like you so much the same."

I stomped into my room yelling in frustration, tore in half the birthday card Amatxi gave me, and set about cleaning up my mess.

When I was done, I found Amatxi on the living room couch napping.

"Finished," I said loud enough to wake her. But Amatxi didn't move. The edge of a pillow partially obscured her face. "Can I have my key now?"

I got no response.

I spotted my motorbike key lying on the floor beside the couch, as if it had fallen out of her hand. I crept forward and snatched up the key. But before I could turn away—eager to be gone—I noticed the silence.

No rattle to Amatxi's breathing; no gentle snoring to her sleep.

"Amatxi?" I touched her hand. Cold.

Dr. Berria later told me she just ran out of breaths. But he never said how.

Dropping the tarp onto the ground, I turn away from the ruined motorbike. I shouldn't have come here. There is no arima to be found. Only broken memories of all the things I've lost.

As I retrace my footsteps toward the house, bats swirl through the night, swooping along the ground in their search for insects. I follow the bats' erratic path with my flashlight beam to a small, dark object lying in the dirt.

A dead bat?

I step closer. It's my father's flip phone. But what is it doing here? Did the phone drop from his pocket as they carried his body away?

I think back to the Christmas I got the phone for him—even though he insisted he didn't need one. Who was he going to call?

"You can call me," I told him when I took the phone out of its box.

"I don't need to call you," Dad said. "You are right here."

"But what if I'm not?" I plugged the phone in to charge. "Say I'm out in the north pasture."

"I will let out my irrintzina."

"What if I'm like in town?" I flipped the phone open and pulled off the protective plastic. "Not even your irrintzina will carry that far."

"Then I'll just wait for you to get back."

I sighed. "Then keep it just in case."

"In case of what?"

"I don't know—in case of an emergency."

Dad shrugged and allowed me to show him the basics of working the phone.

Then he started calling.

First, my father called to tell me the phone worked. Then he called to say it looked like rain. Next call, the barn needed painting. Followed by a call about him wanting a ham sandwich for lunch. Dad called and called and called: the sheep in the pasture were fine; the temperature seemed hotter today than yesterday; now, it no longer looked like rain. Finally, a call letting me know Aitatxi wanted a phone too.

Holy shit.

When my phone rang while cleaning out the barn and I gazed from *Dad* lit up on the screen to Dad standing two feet away, phone pressed to his ear, I threw down my pitchfork. "You need to stop."

"You told me to call you." My father snapped the phone closed.

"Not about every little thing."

"Don't you like talking to me on the phone?"

"What's the point of talking on the phone when I'm standing right here and can talk to you in person?"

Dad pursed his lips. "You listen better when I talk to you on the phone."

Then Aitatxi said he wanted to learn how to text and I ran out of the barn.

I squat down and pick up the phone. What I wouldn't give to have one more annoying phone call from him.

"Xabier?" Idetta clicks on the porch light.

"Coming." I slip Dad's phone in my pocket and hurry toward the light, eager for the warmth of my wife's embrace.

HOLY THURSDAY

...seek, and ye shall find.

MATTHEW 7:7

> > > *counting the flock*

The baby fusses.

He gurgles and chirps from inside his bassinet.

Morning sunlight falls between the slats of the bedroom's shutters to cut lines of light over the floor. I stretch my arms over my head and groan. My right shoulder pops, my lower back aches. I rub sleep from my eyes and stumble over to the bassinet.

When my face appears above him, the baby blinks as if startled: *Where did this guy come from? I was just hanging out and BAM—giant face hovering over me.*

"Good morning." I tickle his belly with my index finger and he laughs, exposing his toothless pink gums. "I bet you're hungry."

When I lift the baby, the lightness of his body sends a tremble through me—my knees buckle. I lean on the bassinet for support. What if I fell? What if I dropped him?

The first time I held my son with his tiny hands and tiny feet, the smallness of him gave me strength. I could do my chores with him tucked in the crook of my arm. For him, I would be a mountain of stone, a protective shield, an impenetrable fortress guarding against the world.

But since my father's accident, I feel more like straw than stone. A stitched-together scarecrow trying to frighten away the circling black birds.

How can I protect my son from a world I no longer understand?

I don't know the answer. All I know is I have a flock to care for and fences to mend, and the sunlight pouring into the room tells me I need to hurry as the day is already running away from me.

I carry the baby to Idetta's side of the bed. With eyes still closed,

Idetta reaches for him. She pulls down her top and has him suckling at her breast before he leaves my arms.

Idetta blinks in the morning light. "Too early."

"Almost seven." I pull on a clean pair of pants, grab a shirt, slip on my boots.

"You want breakfast?"

I shake my head. "I have to make up for the time I lost."

Idetta yawns. "Oh, my Xabier, that is not the way time works."

I am struck by how untrue her words feel. For me, that is *exactly* how time works, slipping away like water through a leaking bucket, and me forever rushing to catch what I've lost before the bucket goes dry.

"Coffee's enough."

"I'll make you a big lunch." Idetta closes her eyes and shifts the baby to her other breast.

I give her a kiss on the cheek—trace the back of my right index finger over the top of my son's head—then steal out the door.

Down in the kitchen, everything has been cleaned up. Except for the red grenadine stain on the tablecloth.

I make myself a cup of instant coffee. Then I scoop a canister of dog food from the bag in the closet and head outside.

The rising sun has already burned all the coolness from the morning. I check the temperature app on my phone—ninety-one for a high. This hot in April means summer will be brutal.

I add *check all pasture water pumps* to my to-do list.

Last summer, when one of the pumps quit, we almost lost half the flock. Luckily we got an early monsoon. The rain bought us enough time to replace the pump and fill the pond.

Dad and I had planned on resealing the bottom of all the ponds right after Easter. We set aside a couple of days to do it; but now, alone, the job will take me at least a week. The five-day forecast shows the temperature retreating into the eighties, which gives me a little window to steal back more time.

I pour dog food into two bowls. "Haugi—Txauri!"

While Haugi rushes over, Txauri stays huddled in front of the barn's closed door.

"Good boy." I run my hands over Haugi's back.

I pick up Txauri's bowl and walk it over to her, sitting it on the ground.

"I know, old girl, I know."

With one hand I scratch Txauri's ears, with the other I touch the wood of the barn. Red flecks of paint stick to my fingers. I wipe them off on the dirt, get to my feet, and continue with my to-do list.

I throw grain over the ground. The chickens rush to peck it up. I break open a fresh bale of hay for the horses, fill their troughs with water, clean out their stalls. A thin layer of moisture coats my arms as I spread a new layer of straw before moving on to the sagging gate leading into the west pasture. I use a rusted pair of pliers to tighten the hinges. The nearly stripped threads of the bolt slip, need replacing. I add it to my to-do list and keep going.

After checking the oil in my truck and adding a quart, I throw the wire stretcher into the truck's bed and drop the tailgate.

"Haugi—Txauri!"

Haugi sprints over and jumps into the bed. Txauri sits up and looks from the barn to me; she barks once, before resettling into the dirt. I get it. I wish I could do the same and just lie down until the weariness and confusion are gone. But then the laughter of my baby boy replays in my ears. I am his mountain fortress, even if I don't feel like it.

After closing the tailgate, I climb into the cab and drive out to check for newborn lambs.

The flock stands bunched together in the far corner of the east pasture. I park my truck and, with Haugi by my side, move into the sheep. The dog keeps his nose to the ground as he pushes his way forward, searching for spots of white nestled on the green. After a half hour, I am relieved we don't find any lambs.

Normally, I would be eager for the lambs to start dropping. New life renewing our flock and ensuring the success of the ranch. But this year, if Aitatxi doesn't get better, taking care of the lambs will all be on me.

Another hole in my bucket of time.

I grab a ewe by the neck. She baaas in protest as I press my hands to her swollen belly. A firm thump strikes my palm. Two days more, three if I'm lucky.

I release the ewe as a car approaches. For a split second I think, *Shit, it's Jenny.* But then the cloud of dust shrouding the car clears and I recognize Fred Big's silver Buick.

He parks behind my truck.

Haugi barks.

Laying a hand on his head, I say, "Enough."

While I am surprised to see Fred out here in the field, I was even more surprised he came to my father's funeral. The two of them weren't exactly friends. That relationship strained when Fred sold his sheep and bought cattle. Then completely severed when Fred committed the unforgivable sin of Americanizing his Basque name, changing it from Ferdinand Bigory to Fred Big.

Even so, because Fred handles the finances for the ranch, he met with Dad once a month. I can only imagine how those encounters went. My father insisting on calling him by his baptismal name, Ferdinand, and Fred having to just smile and help balance the books of a man who, unlike himself, hadn't lost either his name or his ranch.

"Damn it's hot." Fred uses a manila folder for a fan as he waddles toward me—jowls flushing red from exertion.

I nod and, like my father, call him by his birth name, "Morning, Mr. Bigory."

Sunlight glistens off his silver bolo tie. "Xabier, we need to talk."

Right now, standing amid a flock of sheep the day after Dad's funeral, I can't think of a single thing I want to talk to about with a guy my father didn't even like.

Fred points to a nearby oak tree. "Let's borrow some shade."

When we reach the tree, I lean against its trunk. Haugi comes to sit rigidly beside me. The dog scans the sheep, head jerking from side to side with every movement in the flock, as if searching for signs of danger.

But the danger is still a few days off and won't arrive until the coyotes catch the scent of spring lamb blood.

Fred looks across the pasture. "Damn I miss this."

I scratch the top of Haugi's head. "Sweating?"

"Being part of the land."

"Sounds like something my dad would say."

"I will miss your father." Fred wipes sweat from his brow. "He was a constant reminder of all the things I've done wrong in my life."

I blurt out, "Like selling your flock?"

Fred gazes unblinkingly into the distance, and I get the feeling he isn't seeing a flock of sheep grazing in front of him, but a herd of cattle lumbering across the open pasture.

"He told me I was crazy for doing that." Fred shakes his head. "If I'd only waited a few more months—seen the way the economy was turning—who knows what might have happened. Just bad timing. But hell, you can't blame a man for trying to make a better future for his family, now can you?"

Instead of getting satisfaction from him admitting my father was right, my stomach goes queasy. After Fred lost his ranch, his wife left him. She moved to Phoenix and took their daughter with her. Fred missed the better future he was aiming for by over two hundred miles.

I dig the toe of my boot into the grass. "Maybe someday you'll get back into ranching."

Fred pats his belly. "I'm getting a little too fat to have ranching in my future."

Sweat drips from my chin as I think about my father's death and how quickly everything in my life changed. "You never know what the future holds."

"Sometimes you do." Fred's demeanor alters and he's suddenly all business. He taps a finger on the manila folder he carries. "These are the ranch's bank records."

"Dad always took care of that."

"Well, he did and he didn't."

As if sensing danger, the sheep move away from me. Haugi whines—wanting to follow the flock.

Fred hands me the folder. "Ferdinand never said anything?"

The folder is heavier than it appeared; my fingers stick to the outside. "About what?"

"I told him to tell you."

"Tell me what?"

Fred lets out a long, slow breath. "The ranch is in foreclosure."

His words turn the earth liquid beneath my feet. "That's impossible."

Fred avoids eye contact as he lets out a bitter grunt. "The same impossible that happened to me when I lost my ranch."

I steady myself by laying a hand against the trunk of the oak. "But I have a wife—a son."

As if that makes a difference or changes the reality of the situation.

"I know, I know." Fred plops a hand on my shoulder. "That's why there won't be no investigation into what happened."

"Why would you investigate an accident?"

"Standard procedure whenever there's a payout for a life insurance policy."

"What life insurance?"

"Turns out Ferdinand knew how to plan for his family's future better than I did." Fred spits onto the ground. "He went and bought a big policy on himself the day you were born."

› › › *learning a truth*

I pour the contents of the manila folder Fred Big gave me over Aitatxi's bed.

Now that I think about it, the amount of evidence of the ranch being in foreclosure is overwhelming. The busted fences and warping wood; the rusted equipment and broken Farmall.

How did I not see the signs of a ranch in decay?

"Did you know we were in trouble, Aitatxi?" My fingertips cautiously graze the sharp edges of the late notices, unpaid bills, and threatening letters. "Did Dad talk to you about it?"

Aitatxi mumbles something in Euskara.

I put a straw into the smoothie Idetta whipped up in her new Instant Pot. She said it was full of probiotics and antioxidants and all kinds of stuff designed to repair damaged cells. Her concoction is the brownish green of bruised avocados and smells like rotting alfalfa with a splash of chlorine. A whiff of it makes my eyes water.

But Aitatxi seems to like Idetta's smoothie. His lips grab onto the straw and he sucks the liquid into his mouth. His throat constricts as he swallows, eyelids fluttering as if trying to open.

Or maybe it's just a reflex reaction to the shocking taste invading his body.

I remove the straw from his lips and wipe the dribbled remnants of the green liquid off his chin. "You were hungry."

I set the smoothie glass on the nightstand and turn my attention back to the trail of documents leading to the ranch's foreclosure. Amid them lies my father's life insurance policy. A yellowing piece of paper that now holds my future.

"Fred said I didn't need to worry anymore about the foreclosure on the ranch." I press the back of my hand to Aitatxi's forehead—a flicker of warmth moves along my skin. "But what if he's wrong? What if I can't fix all the things that need fixing? If Dad couldn't, how can I?"

Aitatxi rolls onto his side, curls his hands under his chin as if praying. "Maitek gatik pasa nintzazke gauak eta egunak."

Something pings against the bedroom window. I swing my head around so quickly it wrenches my neck. Another pebble hits the glass.

I go to the window. Jean and Louie in cutoffs jump up and down in the bed of Louie's truck, waving six-packs of beer in the air.

I crack a grin. *Dumb Basque-O's.*

My two friends, whooping and hollering below, replace the anvil of dread in my chest with the desire to run from the smell of sour-milk sweat and the sound of labored breathing—to keep the darkness and light of the future nothing but flickering mirages on the horizon.

I rush from the room.

Downstairs, I come to a jolting stop when I find Idetta sitting in the den, bouncing the baby on her knee.

"What's the big hurry?" Idetta asks.

"Jean and Louie are outside."

"Have they come to work?" She's leafing through one of her magazines on kitchen remodeling; the pages are full of clean, white cabinets and shiny metallic appliances, things we don't have money for.

Or didn't. Or might. Or I'm not sure.

I haven't mentioned Dad's life insurance policy to Idetta yet or the ranch being in foreclosure.

I will. Only not now. Later.

Once I've paid off the ranch's debt and secured our home, then I'll tell Idetta everything. Well, maybe not the stuff about Jenny. But everything else she needs to know.

The truck horn honks outside. "I think they want to go swimming."

Idetta's face pinches. "And drink beer?"

The anvil in my chest returns. I don't have time to goof around with my friends. I need to patch the east pasture's barbed-wire fence and start repairing the leaking water ponds.

I slowly exhale. "I'll tell them I have work."

Idetta tilts her head as if something new just occurred to her. "Which do you like better, Hayden, Brayden, or Cayden?"

"Huh?"

"Pascaline likes Hayden. But Maria prefers Brayden. Me, I'm thinking Cayden."

"For what?"

Idetta sighs. "Oh, my Xabier, never mind, just go."

"But I—"

—"Go." Idetta waves me toward the door.

I am out the door before she can change her mind.

› › › *getting a text*

The BOOM of my cannonball reverberates through the water like the recoil of a rifle.

I linger underwater—beneath the pond's undulating surface, the sun wobbles.

My body floats weightless, sealed off from the world. But even here, there is no escape from the past or future as tiny bubbles of air race up and around me, each bubble carrying a new *what if*:

What if something goes wrong with the life insurance payout?

What if there is an investigation?

What if Jenny isn't lying about meeting up with my father?

What if there are more things Dad kept hidden from me?

My *what ifs* scatter as Louie cannonballs right on top of me. His foot catching the side of my head and forcing me to surge upward for air.

"Asshole." I splash water into Louie's face when his head pops up.

"You should have moved out of the way." Louie laughs and splashes me back.

Jean lets out a whoop and crashes into the water between us. When he surfaces, Louie and I join forces and dunk him back under.

Louie, Jean, and I have gone swimming in the south pasture's pond since we could walk. Growing up, the pond was our daily stop after school. The place we bragged about sports, dreamed about girls, and lied about the future: Jean becoming a professional basketball player, Louie traveling the world, and me moving to California.

At the pond was where Jean announced his basketball career was over on account of his damn Basque hands—big, flat palms with stubby fingers—which, according to him, were the sole reason he'd never be an NBA star. Of course, being five foot five and built like a rail tie didn't help. At the pond Louie informed us his travel plans had been put on permanent hold because his girlfriend, Pascaline, was pregnant with twin boys. And it was here where my dream of California evaporated when I told my friends Jenny left without me.

I pop a can of lukewarm Coors. "Who do I owe for the beer?"

Louie shoots Jean a look. "Someone seems to have permanently lost his wallet."

"Lucky for me I have rich friends." Jean raises his can. "To your father, Xabier, the best damn sheep-man in the world."

"The world?" I say.

Jean shrugs. "Our world."

We clank beers.

From the pond, the ranch house is hidden behind a mound of volcanic rock jutting up from the desert. As kids, Louie, Jean, and I pretended the mound was part of a meteor from another planet. Pressing our palms to the warm rock, we swore we could feel the pulse of the aliens trapped inside.

Louie bumps my arm. "Remember the time your dad caught us setting off fireworks behind the barn?"

Jean says, "Or how about when he caught us drinking beers behind the barn?"

I shake my head. "How come we never thought to go any farther away than behind the barn?"

Louie grins. "Because we were dumb Basque-O boys."

We all laugh. But I wonder if we still aren't just *dumb Basque-O boys.*

The three of us gaze into the pond's water, still muddy from our cannonballs. The dull reflection of the sun shimmers on its surface.

Louie throws a stone, shattering the sun and sending chocolate ripples toward the shore. "What are you going to do with the ranch?"

My shoulders tighten at the question. "Work it like always."

"Alone?" Jean says.

"At least until Aitatxi gets better."

We again sit in silence as the ripples die and the pond's surface once more goes flat.

Louie runs his foot through the water. "Remember the toast your dad made at your wedding?"

Jean scowls with concentration. "Something about home and family and sex."

Louie punches Jean in the arm. "It was home and family and children."

Jean punches him back. "Children don't show up without sex."

"My father said, 'Home and family and children are the reason we get married and also the reason we stay married. Here's to Xabier and Idetta finding their reason.'"

"According to Pascaline, home, family, and children aren't the reason she married me." Louie picks up a twig and snaps it in two. "She married me because I had a truck."

Jean scowls. "What does having a truck have to do with marriage?"

"I guess in case she ever wants to leave me, she has something to drive off in."

"Nothing like a woman who can plan ahead," I say.

Jean stretches his arms into the air. "Maria married me because I'm good in bed."

Both Louie and I throw our empty beer cans at him.

"What?" Jean says. "All Basque men are good in bed."

"How would you know?" I reach for another beer.

Jean winks. "Because I'm a Basque man."

Maria marrying Jean because he's a Basque man, leaving out the whole "good in bed" thing, is ironic. Because the first time I met Idetta, she flat out stated she would never marry me precisely because I was a Basque man.

Idetta was one of the Basque dancers from Boise brought in by Urepel's town council to class up our annual Fourth of July picnic. After a performance where two dancers fainted in the 100° plus Arizona heat, everyone crammed into the high school's gym to sip arno gorria.

Everyone except for one girl.

She sat alone at a picnic table in the shade of an oak tree drinking a Picon.

Jenny had been gone to California three months by then. The way it all went down still confused and angered me. Which might have been why I'd been drinking beer like water all day, leaving me drunk and lonely and horny. So I figured, what the hell—this girl might be worth a shot.

As I approached, she fixed her eyes on me. "Keep walking."

"Hello to you too." I sat down across from her.

"Save your 'hello' for some other girl." She took a sip of her drink. "I'm not interested in any Basque man."

"What makes you think I'm interested in any Basque woman?"

"I saw the way you were watching me dance." She flipped back her dark hair. "A wolf is a wolf is a wolf."

"Hey, I just came over to talk." I raised my hands in mock surrender. "No marriage proposal involved."

"Good." She set her drink aside. "Because I would never marry a Basque man."

"Why's that?"

"You're stubborn, secretive, and mistake grunting for speech."

"Ugh, sometime me use big word."

That brought the hint of a smile to her soft, full lips.

"If you don't like Basque men, what the hell are you doing at a Basque picnic full of us?"

"My ama's head of the dance squad." She nodded toward a woman lingering near the gym's door and wearing the same traditional Basque dancers red skirt as her. "This whole Basque dancing thing makes her happy."

"So you only came to Urepel to make your ama happy?"

"What can I say, I'm a good daughter." She folded her arms across her chest. "Now go away."

"What's your name?"

"Nope."

"Maybe I'll just ask your ama."

She turned her face directly toward me—her features sharp and clear. "Now what fun would that be?"

"So you do want to have some fun?"

"Not the fun you're thinking of."

"Give me your number."

She raised a skeptical eyebrow. "So you can drunk-text me, no thanks."

"C'mon, give me a chance."

Instead of shooting me down with another clever comment, this girl eyed me like I was a melon whose ripeness she was trying to determine.

I sat up straighter and ran a quick hand through my hair.

Finally, she sighed and then, like it was utterly against her better judgement, said, "Go get a pen."

I jumped up and ran. When I returned, she grabbed my hand and wrote on my palm.

I scowled when I read what she'd written. "What's this?"

"My address."

"But it's in Boise."

"You thought I'd be easy?"

"Easier," I said as I calculated how many hours it would take to drive to and from Idaho.

"You can knock on my door when you sober up." She smoothed the front of her skirt. "If you want."

"You still haven't told me your name."

"Guess you'll have to come to Boise and find out." Then she

got up and, before walking away, added, "Just remember, I'm never going to marry a Basque man."

Twenty-five trips to Boise and four months later, she did.

My cell phone dings.

Jean whistles. "Someone's in trouble."

Louie slips on his shirt. "Recess is over."

Like him, I think it's Idetta texting me to come home. But instead, my stomach sours at the sight of Jenny's number.

There are no words to her text. Only the picture of a crumbled receipt from a Holiday Inn coffee shop in Kingman. The receipt is signed *Ferdinand Etxea*, and dated three days before my father died.

››› *starting a fight*

On the drive back from the pond, I roll my phone over and over in my hand—the image of the coffee shop receipt burning into my palm.

I again examine the receipt's signature, to be sure the angle of the *E* and the cross of the *t* belong to my father.

It's just a receipt. A stupid piece of paper. Only how did Jenny get it?

As we pull up to the ranch house, Dr. Berria's green Jeep is driving away.

A layer of sweat flushes over my skin—*Aitatxi?*

I jump from Louie's truck and run into the house, expecting chaos and tears and death. But instead I'm greeted by Idetta calmly sitting at the kitchen table with the baby. Cardboard boxes of fried fish, coleslaw, and French fries are spread out over the tabletop.

"What's going on?"

The baby sits in his highchair, chewing on his rattle. He bangs the rattle on the highchair's tray and giggles as if each blow is too amusing to be ignored.

"Dr. Berria brought us dinner." Idetta scoops a spoonful of coleslaw onto her paper plate.

"He drove all the way out here just for that?"

"He was coming out anyway to check on Aitatxi." Idetta puts a handful of French fries alongside her coleslaw. "So I asked him to swing by the church's fish fry on his way."

"Why didn't you tell me he was coming?"

"You were busy." Idetta doesn't look at me when she says this, and I get the same unsettled feeling in my stomach as when she bought the new Instant Pot. The appliance just showing up on the counter. Idetta off-handedly saying it was on sale. Only the tone of her voice and cast of her gaze letting me know it probably wasn't. Nothing worth starting a fight over. Just an appliance. Yet my wife's little deception lingered like cobwebs nestled in a corner that sooner or later needed to be cleared away.

I let go of my grip on the doorknob. "You didn't want me here."

"Sit down and eat, Xabier."

"That's why you let me go with Louie and Jean."

Idetta gives the baby a French fry. "I needed to speak with Dr. Berria alone."

I take the French fry away from the baby and toss it into the sink. "So you lied to me?"

My own string of deceptions turns the words bitter in my mouth. Including Jenny's coffee shop receipt, which I have no intention of telling Idetta about. Why should I? The text has nothing to do with Idetta. Maybe nothing to do with anything and just Jenny's way of tormenting me. But why would she do that? She left; I stayed. I pinch the bridge of my nose.

Stop thinking about Jenny.

Idetta fixes her gaze on me. "I didn't tell you, Xabier, because you aren't seeing things clearly."

I shut the door and step fully into the kitchen. "He's my aitatxi."

"And this is my family."

"What does that mean?"

"Aitatxi needs more than we can give him."

"He's getting better." I put my hands flat on the table and lean forward. "He drank all that stuff you made him and his skin feels warmer and he tried to open his eyes and—"

—"Stop, Xabier." Idetta grabs my hand. "You need to face the fact Aitatxi no longer wants to be here."

I pull my hand from hers. "Here?"

"You know what I mean."

The kitchen goes silent. Even the baby quits banging his rattle.

And it's like the quiet before a monsoon hits, when the world turns still and the air swells with what is to come, but not yet here—the moment before everything changes.

I exhale. "I won't give up hope."

"Oh, my Xabier, it's not about hope—it's about reality." Idetta leans back in her chair. "We can't—I can't—keep taking care of Aitatxi."

Her words stun me. Because instead of hearing Idetta's *can't*, I hear her unsaid *won't*.

"Then I'll take care of my aitatxi by myself."

"And what about the ranch? The flock? You can't do it all on your own, Xabier."

I clench my jaw. "I can—I will."

Idetta takes several deep breaths. "Dr. Berria said, we need to start thinking about moving him to a facility."

"Facility?"

"A nursing home." Idetta plows forward. "It would be the best place for him."

"To what? Die?"

"Dr. Berria said we can wait until after Easter, but then—"

—"No!" I bang my hand on the table, sending French fries, coleslaw, and fish to the floor.

The baby starts to cry, and Idetta picks him up as the kitchen door swings open and Louie sticks his head in. "Everything okay?"

Idetta bounces the baby on her knee. "Everything is fine, Louie."

I want to say, *Everything is not fine, everything will never be fine again.* But anger takes away my words. The air in the room is suddenly scorching—like I'm standing beneath the sun in an open field with no shade in sight.

I brush past Louie and out onto the porch.

The setting sun bathes the world in yellows and oranges. Jean sits on the passenger side of Louie's truck drinking a beer. He raises his can to me and grins.

Louie comes to stand beside me. "What the hell was that about?"

"I don't know."

My thoughts come thick and slow. My head still fuzzy from the alcohol. I glance at the kitchen door, opening and closing my hands, fingers bloated, palms stinging as if I rubbed them over splintered wood.

"This have anything to do with Jenny?" Louie asks.

"What? No."

"You can tell me if something is going on."

"Idetta and I just had a fight. It happens."

"Okay, buddy." Louie pats me on the back. "Call me if you need anything."

I nod as Louie walks to his truck and climbs in.

As my friends drive away, the yellows and oranges of the day give way to the red of dusk. I head back inside. Idetta and the baby are no longer in the kitchen. Only the remains of the un-eaten meal, scattered over the floor.

› › › *sending a text*

The ding of my phone wakes me.

The room so dark I'm not sure if my eyes are open or closed. Am I awake? Or still dreaming of *the flock running wildly through a flooded pasture, fleeing a pack of coyotes, and Dad standing knee-deep in the water, panicked sheep splashing and baaing as they race past him; he calls to me from where I linger at the edge of the pasture, "Don't lose your arima, Xabier." But I am confused and don't know what I am supposed to be hoping for.*

My phone dings again. The screen ignites.

I roll onto my side. I can't shake off the fogginess of sleep; it rolls in thick clouds through my head and swells in my chest, urging me to let go and fall back into my watery dream. I blindly reach over to the nightstand and grab my phone. Pull it right up to my face—*Jenny.*

That brings me awake.

I instinctively glance over my shoulder at Idetta. After I cleaned up the kitchen, I lingered downstairs until I was sure both she and the baby were asleep. Not having the energy for another fight.

Idetta lets out a soft snore, followed by a muffled word as she shifts onto her side.

I slip out of bed and with my phone in hand tiptoe from the room.

Moonlight falls through the window at the end of the hallway to illuminate the wood floor in sheets of uneven light. I close the bedroom door and move into that light as I read Jenny's text: *You've seen the receipt—we need to talk.*

I delete it and stare at the black screen of my phone.

Could *he* have really been seeing *her?*

No way. Impossible. Damn receipt.

Since I'm up, I decide to check on Aitatxi, whose room is located at the end of the hall, right next to Dad's.

The floor creaks with my every step. I walk slow, deliberate, like I am unsure of my footing and where I am headed. Then, as if of their own accord, my feet stop in front of Dad's room.

I haven't been inside since the morning last May when he didn't come to breakfast and I went to check on him, knocking gently and calling, "Dad?" When he didn't answer, I pushed open the door to find him sitting in his underwear on the edge of the bed, staring out the window; his bent back and gray hair so much like Aitatxi.

"You okay?"

My father ran a hand over his face as if wiping away the remnants of a bad dream. "Everything's fine."

Only it wasn't fine—not then and not now. I linger with my hand on the cold steel of the doorknob. This is my father's place, not mine. Or it *was* his. But he's gone and I'm left to deal with...what?

Uncertainty causes me to push open the door.

As I step into my father's bedroom, the smell of my mother's perfume moves over me and darkness becomes light and she is again there and smiling and reaching a hand from where she lies in bed, beckoning me to sit with her and talk for a few minutes.

I hesitate in the doorway as my waking dream fades.

As a boy, my nightmares held the Mamu, the Basque version of Bigfoot. Whenever I misbehaved, Aitatxi told me how the Mamu—who was forever hiding and lurking and watching by the woodpile outside—had a taste for naughty boys.

When I was good, the Mamu's appetite seemed to wane.

Even though I told Aitatxi I didn't believe in the Mamu, at night I pulled my blanket up around my neck and stared unblinkingly at the window to be sure the Mamu didn't sneak in.

I'd forgotten the Mamu. At least until I opened this door and found him still hiding and lurking and waiting—nightmares no longer confined to the dreams of my youth.

I step into the room and click on the nightstand lamp.

A circle of light spreads over the half-made bed. On the far side, the sheets are rumpled and the blanket pushed back. The pillow lies at an angle and holds the impression of my father's head.

On the side of the bed nearest me, the blanket is smooth, edges tucked beneath the mattress. The pillow unused.

Embarrassment heats the back of my neck. I shouldn't be here. I wouldn't be—not if Dad was alive.

Next to the lamp on the nightstand sits a nearly empty bottle of Mom's perfume. I breathe in the bouquet of artificial roses rising from her side of the bed.

Did Dad spray Mom's perfume on her pillow each night? Close his eyes and let himself believe she was still here? Drift off to sleep with his wife winding her way into his dreams?

My phone dings. Another text from Jenny. I press delete without reading it and move to the dresser.

In the top drawer, I discover more bank documents along with the ledger for the ranch. I slide my finger down the numbers written inside—every month ending in red.

In the next drawer down, I find a rawhide pouch bound by a strap of leather. I lay it on top of the dresser. Undoing the tie, I unroll the rawhide to reveal a set of worn chisels. The buttery scent of aged leather brings back summer days spent in the barn with wood chips clinging to my sweating skin; Aitatxi's hands firmly guiding mine as we used a hammer to gently chisel a repeating pattern in the wood.

I slide out a chisel. Press my fingers along its shaft, down to the scalloped edge of its tip.

So this is where Dad put Aitatxi's wood-carving tools. Saving them for what? To one day give back to Aitatxi so he could start carving again? Or is this a piece of the past to be forever hidden in a drawer?

I return the chisel to the pouch and retie the leather strap.

As I place the wood-carving tools back in the drawer, I spot the book. Thin and worn. The pages curled. Robert Laxalt's *In a Hundred Graves*.

I pick up the book Mom gave Dad for his birthday so many years ago.

On the inside cover are the words *For My Love*.

As I turn the page, a folded sheet of paper falls from the book. On it, two lines written by Dad—

For my loved ones I would pass nights and days;
Nights and days, deserts and woods.

The top of the paper is dated a week before he died.

My phone dings.

Jenny again: *Meet me tomorrow at the holiday inn coffee shop from the receipt.*

Delete.

Returning the sheet of paper to the book, I place the book next to the carving tools and close the dresser drawer.

As I turn to leave, I spot the Instant Pot box set just inside the bedroom door.

Damn it—Idetta bought another Instant Pot and hid it inside my father's room, sure I wouldn't come in here and find it.

Only now I have.

My head swells with pressure—each beat of my heart reverberating in my temples.

If Idetta wants to play that game, then I'll just do something without telling her—well, something more. I'll take the new Instant Pot out of the box and throw it in the garbage and leave the empty box for her to find.

But when I yank open the top, instead of finding another shiny appliance, I discover my father's metal wristwatch and leather wallet; his silver lauburu ring and the black flip phone I found in the dirt.

Dark speckles of dried blood cover the glass face of the watch, the leather of the wallet, the silver of the lauburu. But no blood mars the blackness of the phone.

Idetta must have found the phone in my pants pocket while doing the laundry. She put the phone in the box with the rest of Dad's things and stowed the box away, knowing I wasn't ready for what it held.

I am one dumb Basque-O.

A ding comes from inside the Instant Pot box, and my father's cell phone lights up.

I kneel—my face washed in the glow of the phone's light. I can't seem to pull enough air into my lungs—because even though it's crazy and stupid and impossible, I let myself hope—*Dad sending me a message.*

With shaking hands, I lift the phone out of the box as if it is no longer just a phone I bought on sale at Walmart but a rare artifact—a conduit to a different world. I flip open the phone: MORTGAGE OVERDUE NOTICE.

My body sags. Enough self-torture for one night. Time to get back to bed. Morning will be here before I know it with more things added to my to-do list.

Before I replace the phone in the Instant Pot box, even though it's none of my business, I scroll down to Dad's call history. The last phone call he made minutes before he died was to a number forever ingrained in my memory.

I collapse onto my haunches as I close his phone. Then I set it back in the box next to his watch and wallet and lauburu. I text Jenny: *Be there at 9.*

GOOD FRIDAY

*For Jonas three days and three nights in the whale's belly;
so shall the Son of man be three days and
three nights in the heart of the earth.*

MATTHEW 12:40

››› *making a list*

I wake before sunrise and slip silently out of bed in order not to wake Idetta. I want to avoid another argument with my wife— which will happen if she asks me how Aitatxi's doing, and I say, "Don't worry, he'll be dead soon enough." Or if she calls my son Jayden or Hayden or some other made-up Generation Z name. Or if I tell her I'm going to meet up with my ex-fiancée.

Even though I'm only going to talk to Jenny because I have questions. Like how the hell she got tangled up with my father— and just how tangled up were they?

The whole thing is disturbing.

Also, I don't trust Jenny. I mean, really, after everything between us, why should I?

All the stuff with Jenny and me took place a lifetime ago. Back when I was naïve and thought when people made a commitment to each other they meant it.

The only reason I agreed to see her now is because I need answers.

Only, if I try to explain that to Idetta, well...if she can't understand about Aitatxi, my wife sure as hell isn't going to understand me meeting up with an old flame who I've conveniently avoided ever talking to her about.

There is no sense in getting Idetta worked up over nothing. Only why then do I have this queasy feeling that avoiding an argument with my wife isn't the sole reason I'm sneaking out of bed?

I should wake Idetta and tell her where I'm going and try to get her to understand. But I don't. Because I finally get why Aitatxi waited so long for the right time to say hello to Amatxi. Right now is not the time for me to say hello or anything else to Idetta.

As I slip from the bedroom, the five thousand miles once separating my grandparents feels like nothing compared to the distance between my wife and me.

In the kitchen, I grab a cup of coffee. Then I go outside and sit on the porch steps.

Early morning shadows give way to streaks of orange and red. The colors wash out to yellow as they spread over the land to illuminate fences and sheep, desert and pasture. The air tinged with alfalfa from broken hay bales and salty dust kicked up by the flock; the pungent scent of creosote bushes and fresh manure mix with the smell of chickens and horses and sheep—all the familiar odors of the ranch—over which floats the mossy sweetness of the Colorado River.

As a boy, I sat on the porch steps with Dad—him drinking coffee, me drinking milk with a splash of coffee in it—while he made his to-do list for the day. He would number the things he needed to get done, repeat them, change the order slightly, add to the details. Then Dad would recite the entire list aloud—like a kind of prayer—in the hope that by nightfall everything on the list would be completed.

When I think of the list of things I need to do today, it feels more like a curse than a prayer.

1. Avoid fighting with Idetta.
2. Not give up on Aitatxi.
3. Get ready for the lambs to drop (which has a whole subset list of its own).
4. Find out what Jenny does or doesn't know.
5. Check in with Fred about the life insurance payout.

I sigh and say, "That's quite a to-do list you left me, Ferdinand."

Saying my father's name aloud makes me think of my son. Now more than ever I want to name him Ferdinand. Not only as a way to keep a part of Dad alive, but as a way to claim the name that at twelve I learned was almost mine.

"I wanted to name you Ferdinand, but your father wouldn't let me," Mom told me as I sat on the bed beside her. Even though her cancer kept her mostly bedridden and nearly all of her hair had fallen out, I believed my mother was getting better. Fewer visits to the hospital. Not as many bottles of pills on her nightstand. Soon she'd be up making me sourdough pancakes for breakfast.

"Ferdinand?" The movement of the name over my lips suddenly felt different, weighed down by the thought of who I might have been. *Ferdinand.* Could a name change a person? Who they were? What they did? "How come he didn't want me to have his name?"

"Your father wanted you to be special."

"Dad isn't special?"

"Of course he is, but Ferdinand wanted you to be *more* special than him."

"Why?"

"That's the way it is with fathers." Mom's voice was no more than a whisper, making everything sound like a secret just between the two of us. "They want their sons to be better than them and do things they never could. You are his dream come to life."

Dad would never say something like that to me. Dreams were Mom's realm. After she was gone, the conversations I had with my father never strayed far from things we could hammer or mow, shear or cut. Mom was the bridge from dreams to reality. An expanse whose width Dad and I couldn't cross on our own.

So, instead of being named after my father, I got my name from Saint Francis Xavier, a Basque founder of the Jesuits. Spelled with a *b* instead of a *v* because that was the way the town Saint Francis came from spelled it.

I bit the corner of my lip. "I wish I were Ferdinand."

"Xabier is a good name." My mother lowered her chin as she raised an eyebrow. "A saint's name."

I kicked the bed frame. "I don't want to be a saint."

"Not something I think you need to worry about." Mom pressed her lips together and nodded. "You just concentrate on being Xabier."

"I can do that."

I glanced out the window. Dad and Aitatxi were loading hay into the back of a truck while Amatxi gathered vegetables from the garden. The school bus would be arriving any moment. Mom and I had only a few more minutes together.

She shifted in her bed and sat up straighter. "Remember when I used to tell you stories before bed?"

"I liked those."

"Me too." She cleared her throat. "Remember the story about the lamiak?"

"The little people who come into the house when we're sleeping?"

"That's right."

"Which is kind of creepy."

"Maybe a little." Mom folded her hands. "Do you remember what happens to the lamiak?"

"They always break stuff—a lamp or chair—and can't figure out how to fix it."

"More or less." Mom's laughter trailed into a coughing fit that rattled her body. I handed her the glass of water on the night-stand and held my breath until the coughing stopped and everything became good again. She cleared her throat. "The point is sometimes in life things get broken, Xabier, and like the lamiak, no matter how we try, they can't be fixed."

"Dad can fix anything," I said. "He even rebuilt the genera-tor in the barn."

"I'm sorry, Xabier." My mother took my hand; the coldness of her fingers startled me. "But your father can't fix what is broken in me."

I pulled my hand away. "I've got to catch the bus."

"Xabier, you need to understand—"

—"I don't want to be late for school."

"Xabier, I just—"

But before she could utter another word, I ran from the bedroom—sprinted through the house—and burst out onto the porch shaking off the tears rimming my eyes.

Then, like Dad with his to-do list, I prayed. "Mom will get better. Her hair will grow back. She will live."

I believed those things as I sprinted to the waiting bus. Because I was a boy who thought the future he wanted would be the future he got.

I finish my coffee and set the cup on the porch steps. Then I get up and stride toward my truck—a man who knows wanting isn't enough.

› › › *breaking a heart*

When I walk into the Holiday Inn coffee shop, the lady behind the register wearing a *Hi, I'm Alice* name tag, smacks her lips together. "You look like your dad."

Her words cause my face to burn.

"This way." Alice leads me to the back of the coffee shop where Jenny sits in a booth, sipping Coke through a straw.

"I'm sorry about Ferdinand." Alice puts a coffee cup on the table. "He was a good tipper. Black?"

I nod and slide into the booth.

"Just like Dad," Alice says as she pours me a cup.

When she moves on to another table, I ask, "How does she know my father?"

"This is where we met every week."

"You and my dad?"

Jenny nods. "Our booth."

"Your booth?"

"He sat right where you're sitting every Tuesday." Jenny smiles brightly like she is revealing some wonderful secret, having nothing to do with death and loss and the confusion about both that brought me here.

I shift my weight; the booth's wooden frame presses into my spine. "I don't see it."

And I literally don't. I can't picture Dad in this place. Not just in this Holliday Inn café smelling of cinnamon or in this sticky vinyl booth, but *here* across from my ex-fiancée.

"I ran into him at the Walmart in Kingman." Jenny gives her head a decisive nod, as if Walmart somehow adds validity to her story.

I clasp my coffee cup so that the heat burns my palms. None of this makes sense. My father never seemed to like Jenny, and once said she wasn't right for me. Now Jenny is sitting here wanting me to believe she somehow became right for him?

"Ferdinand was in the hardware aisle."

Hearing Jenny call my father by his first name unsettles me even more. He was always Mr. Etxea to Jenny. Apparently, at least according to her, all that changed.

"Ferdinand was buying a hammer for the ranch and I needed some tools to put together my new bed." Jenny tucks her blonde hair behind her ears. "It was a little awkward at first—I mean, after everything between you and me. But then he started asking me all about why I was back in Arizona and what happened with Los Angeles and—"

—"Why are you back in Arizona, and what happened with Los Angeles?"

Jenny's face flushes. "Not that it's any of your business, but Los Angeles wasn't the right fit for me."

"Like Urepel wasn't?" I say, but really mean *like I wasn't?*

"That's the past, Xabier." Jenny's eyes lock onto mine. "I'm here to talk about the future—our future."

"Ours?"

"That's right," Jenny says. "Mine here in Kingman and yours—"

—"On the ranch."

Jenny smirks. "Some things never change."

"They sure don't."

"Anyway, Ferdinand being so friendly kind of surprised me." Jenny sits up straighter. "Because, well, he never talked to me much back when we dated. But he asked me for my phone number and we started texting." Jenny giggles. "Ferdinand loved to text and he was so funny."

My dad? Funny?

"Anyway, one thing led to the next, and we started meeting up weekly for coffee."

"You mean sex." I say it to shock Jenny and throw her off whatever game she's playing.

"I mean coffee."

"Which is code for sex."

"Don't be an ass, Xabier." Jenny kicks me under the table. "Ferdinand needed someone to talk to."

"And he chose you because you're such a great conversationalist?"

"He chose me because I'm a good listener."

"Somehow I don't remember that."

Jenny places her hands flat on the table. "This isn't about us, Xabier—it's about Ferdinand."

I let out a disparaging grunt—*like I could forget that.*

Two booths over, a man about my father's age sits with a woman whose dark hair is streaked with gray. He wears a plaid shirt and green John Deere cap; his hands are weathered from working outside. The woman's eyes light up when she laughs at something he says. The man reaches across the table and covers her hand with his. And I wonder, How well do they know each other? Have they been married for years? Or is this just a once-a-week hookup? Their relationship as temporary as the coffee I drink?

I rip open a packet of sugar and dump it into my cup. "So what did you talk about?"

"Mostly you."

I swallow the bile rising in my throat. Now I know she's lying. Because my father would never choose Jenny to discuss my life with. He wouldn't betray me like that.

She reaches across and touches my hand. "I'm here to help, Xabier."

I pull my hand away. "Help who?"

"You and me."

"Just how you going to do that?"

"By letting you know what Ferdinand wanted."

74

The urge to get up and walk out of the café and block Jenny's number and cut her from my life for good this time courses through me. But I came here to find out what she thinks she knows about what happened to my father. I just didn't expect to hear details about the two of them being together—in whatever way they were.

"Tell me," I say.

Jenny takes in her moment of victory before saying, "Ferdinand felt guilty about what was happening with the bank and believed it was all his fault. I told him it wasn't. But, well, Ferdinand could be hardheaded."

"Don't call him that."

"Hardheaded?"

"Ferdinand."

"Fine." Jenny folds her arms across her chest. "Your dad was worried about you."

I let out a huff. "Why?"

"He didn't think you could handle losing the ranch."

I clasp my hands together like I'm praying, and maybe I am. Praying that every word out of her mouth is a lie. "He never mentioned any of this to me."

"He said he tried."

I search my memories but can find no missed moment, no unfinished sentence, no awkward silence.

Jenny licks her lips. "He wanted to protect you."

I slump in the booth. If what Jenny is saying is true—and that's a big "if"—it meant my father still thought of me as a boy who needed protecting and not a man who could handle the truth.

I unclasp my hands and lay them palms up on the table. "If you were so concerned about my father, why didn't you tell me what was going on?"

"Would you have believed me?"

"No."

"Finally, some honesty." Jenny puts her elbows on the tabletop. "Here's a little more—you never intended to go with me to California."

The skin of my forehead pinches; I click my tongue. "I thought this wasn't about us."

"I'm sick of being the bad guy in our breakup." Jenny chews on a lock of her hair, just like she did on our first date, when we went to a football game and it took me until the fourth quarter to work up enough courage to slide my hand over hers. "I did us both a favor by leaving like I did."

"So you broke my heart for my own good?"

"I had to go."

"If you would have just given me time—"

—"For what?" Jenny shakes her head. "You were never going to pull the trigger and that's the truth."

What Jenny says isn't the truth, at least not for me. I intended to create a future with her in California. Get married—have children. I just needed a little more time to figure things out. But Jenny was always in a such a big hurry—rushing toward the future—and me just a dumb Basque-O to believe *my* dream of the future was ever *hers*.

"What do you want from me, Jenny?"

The smug smile returns to her face. "Ferdinand told me about his life insurance policy."

Sweat slides down my back. "Why would he do that?"

"To make sure you and I both got the future he wanted for us."

"And what future is that?"

"Me a new start in Kingman and you to keep your precious ranch." Jenny leans back in her seat "That's why he did it."

"What?" I push my coffee cup away. "Die in an accident?"

Jenny's gaze bores like a shaft of rebar into my skull. "What happened in the barn wasn't an accident."

All the blood seems to drain out of me—as though I too am being crushed by a tractor. "What are you talking about?"

"Ferdinand couldn't figure out any other way to save the ranch except with his life insurance policy."

Understanding of what Jenny says trickles into me. I want to scream and yell and let her know her truth is a lie. But my throat constricts and all I can think about are Fred Big's words—"There won't be no investigation." Suddenly the unsaid *why* of those words takes on new meaning.

"Did you know?"

"We talked and I—"

—I slap my hand on the table. "Did you know!"

The older couple at the nearby table glance over. Alice walks up with a pot of coffee in her hand.

"Everything all right?" She glances from me to Jenny and back. "More coffee?"

"I think he's had enough coffee," Jenny says in a calm, even voice. "Could you get me a Coke to go, Alice?"

"Sure, honey."

After Alice is gone, Jenny scowls at me. "If I'd have known, don't you think I would have stopped him?"

"You tell me."

"I cared about Ferdinand, Xabier." On cue, Jenny's eyes tear up. "He helped me—we helped each other."

"And now he's dead."

"That is not on me."

I lean back as the heat in me dissipates. "No, it's not."

"I'm glad you can see that." Jenny takes a pen from her purse, jots something down on a napkin and slides it over. The dollar amount written on the napkin runs like a jagged corkscrew through my body.

"What's this?"

"There's no reason anyone else needs to know about what really happened in that barn." Jenny leans toward me. "His life insurance policy is no good if the cause of death was suicide."

Suicide? The word pulls all the warmth out of me. I shiver. "How do you know?"

Jenny pulls her hair into a ponytail and secures it with a tie. "I checked."

"So you're blackmailing me over my father's death?"

"We had plans—Ferdinand made promises." Jenny points to the napkin. "He would have wanted me to have the money."

I shake my head in disgust. "What happened to you?"

"I grew up—you should try it." Jenny slides from the booth. "Let me know when the life insurance policy pays out."

"And if I don't?"

"Well then, Xabier, neither us of will be getting the future we want."

› › › having Basque hands

Driving back to Urepel, my hands are not my own. Someone else's fingers grip the wheel. Steering toward an unknown destination with no map. All because Jenny said the loss of my father was not just a terrible accident—but something else.

Like my hands, my body is not mine either. In a truck, on a road, no longer leading toward the future but only away from the past. And me? Well, I'm the dumb Basque-O trapped inside, yelling and screaming and hoping for a way out.

The truck rattles as it bumps over a pothole. Through the bug-splattered windshield rising waves of heat blur the horizon.

I bang the hand—which is not mine—against the steering wheel. Pain shoots up my arm like the closing wire of a snare, yanking me back to the week before Dad died when he told me what Basque hands are good for.

We stood along the edge of the north pasture where lacewings flittered in a chaotic dance through the sun's fading light. I held my son while Dad worked the fence stretcher.

I'd been patching fence with my father since I was ten years old. He taught me how to put the two strands of broken wire in either end of the stretcher and pump the handles until the strands overlapped and could be spliced together. Back then, it took me nearly thirty minutes and a lot of sweat to fix a single busted wire. Now—having stretched thousands of feet of barbed wire—fixing a break only takes a couple of minutes.

"What's for dinner?" Dad twisted the broken ends of the barbed wire together.

"Aitatxi is showing Idetta how to make cassoulet."

Dad grunted. "I'll check the barn's refrigerator for leftovers."

Every now and then, Aitatxi instructed Idetta on how to make one of the meals his ama cooked for him as a boy in Euskal Herria. But Aitatxi had never actually made any of the dishes—only eaten them. As such, what he remembered and what turned out were often culinarily incompatible.

Frozen leftovers became our regular backup.

"I think there's some lemon chicken from last week." I settled my son into the crook of my left arm.

Dad nodded and hung the fence stretcher on a post. A low blanket of dust moved over the pasture and came to swirl around our feet as the day's lingering heat was washed away on a cool breeze from the unseen river.

Dad held out a little finger. The baby wrapped his hand around it and gurgled. "He's got Basque hands."

"All palms and short stubby fingers?"

"Hands good for holding on to things."

"What things?"

My father's gaze moved across the land. "This."

"He'd have to have really big hands to hold on to the whole ranch."

"He doesn't have to hold on to all of it at once." Dad kissed the top of the baby's head. "Just a piece at a time."

I chuckled. "If you say so, Dad."

Mourning doves descend from the darkening sky to land in the pasture. The birds settled into the grass to roost for the night—their cooing haunted the air.

"Dinner probably ready," I said.

Dad nodded. "We should go."

Only we didn't move.

We just stood there, three generations of Etxeas, lingering in the glow of sunset and making use of our Basque hands to hold on—me to my son, and my son to my father.

When I reach Urepel's downtown, I park in front of Fred Big's office. The sign reads: *Sheriff-Banker-Real Estate-Insurance Agent Specialist.*

I let go of the steering wheel and turn off the truck as my hands again become my own—large flat palms and short thick fingers. Basque hands, good for holding on, which is exactly what I intend to use them for.

I push open the door and step out onto the asphalt. A car honks as it passes. Claire Bidarte waves. She lost her husband, Pierre, in an accident five years ago; he fell off the roof of his barn while making repairs. Only now do I wonder why Pierre was on the roof alone. How come his brother, John, wasn't up there helping?

Damn Jenny.

Marcelino Ugalde calls my name from across the street. He waves as he slips into Benji's Café. Maybe I should have parked around back or in the adjacent alley. But why? Fred was my father's lawyer—or at least the closest thing to a lawyer in Urepel—so why wouldn't I be going to his office?

A bell clanks as I enter. The room is empty.

"Hello?" The place seems more like a stable barn than an office—littered with cow horns, horse saddles, and lasso ropes. Fred recreating the scenario of a life he no longer lives.

On his oversized wooden desk sits a picture of him with my dad in their twenties. They stand in a pasture, arms around each other's shoulders. There's not enough detail visible in the background to tell where the picture was taken—our ranch or Fred's.

Has the picture always been here?

Did my father see it every time he came to go over the books or to ask about the foreclosure?

A reminder of their lost friendship?

Or did Fred find the picture after the funeral, crammed into a forgotten box, and put it on his desk as a memorial to the past?

A toilet flushes. Fred steps from the bathroom.

"Well, hey there Xabier." Fred closes the bathroom door behind him. "I was just going to give you a call."

I pick up the picture of him and Dad. "Where was this taken?"

"By the river." Fred slides into the chair behind his desk. "Back before your aitatxi learned that parcel was no good for ranching. You know, I offered to buy it from him a while ago to put a warehouse on. But he said your amatxi wouldn't like that."

"Amatxi always dreamed of building a new house there."

"Well, dreams have a way coming and going."

I set the picture back down. "Why were you going to call me?"

"I need your signature to file the life insurance claim." Fred pulls some papers from his desk's top drawer.

I take a seat across from him. "Will there be enough money to save the ranch?"

"Just enough." Fred gives me a pen and slides a paper over to me.

I give the paper a quick scan and sign it. "Holding on to the ranch is all that matters."

"You know, this is just a Band-Aid, Xabier." Fred leans back in his chair. "The ranch has been losing money for years. It's not going to be easy to change that."

"I'll find a way."

"That's what Ferdinand said." Fred slides another piece of paper in front of me.

"What's this?"

"The second life insurance policy."

My name appears at the top. "I don't get it."

"The day you graduated college, Ferdinand came in here and insisted I write up a life insurance policy on you."

"Why would he do that?"

"He was your father, you tell me."

I take a deep breath. My father. A man full of things left unsaid. I exhale slowly. "What am I supposed to do with it?"

"Take it with you, read it over, let me know if you have any questions."

82

"I, uh, was wondering about something." I fold the policy up and cram it into my back pocket. "About how you said there won't be any investigation into the accident."

"That's right."

"But if there was." I tap my fingers on the edge of the desk. "What would it be about?"

"Just an examination of the physical evidence in the barn." Fred folds his hands and appraises me. "Why you asking?"

Before I can think of a lie to put him off, the bell to his office clanks, and Jenny walks in.

"Well I'll be—" Fred gets to his feet—"Jenny Wheeler back in Urepel after all these years."

"Hi Mr. Big." Jenny beams a smile at Fred and then turns it on me. "Hey there, Xabier. Funny seeing you here."

Fred gives Jenny a big hug. "I didn't get a chance to talk to you at the funeral."

"I wasn't there long." Jenny places a hand on my right shoulder. "Didn't even tell Xabier how sorry I am about his father's accident."

Every muscle in my body tightens as she says the word she claims is a lie. The word she threatened to replace with another word. I stare straight ahead—still caught in the snare of the past and unsure how to escape.

I stand. "I gotta get back to the ranch."

Jenny digs her fingernails into my shoulder. "But Xabier, we have so much to catch up on."

I shrug off her grip. "I have to go."

"I'll call you when everything is settled," Fred says. "A week, maybe two."

"Fine." I walk out the door.

Outside, I blink in the bright sunshine as my heart pounds like I've just sprinted across an open pasture.

As the office bell clanks behind me, I head toward my truck.

But before I can get the door open, Jenny grabs on to my arm and jerks me around to face her. "What the hell do you think you're doing?"

When I spot Jessie Camino's black truck heading toward us, I pull Jenny into the shadows of the adjacent alley.

Jenny laughs. "So now we're meeting in secret?"

"Quit following me."

"I didn't have to follow you." Jenny flicks back her hair. "You're so predictable."

"Leave me alone," I say, but there is no force to my words.

"I won't let you blow this for us, Xabier."

"Us?"

"Yeah, us." Jenny leans against the side of Fred's office building. "I plan on using the money to start a new life—you can have one too."

"I already have a life."

"I know you want more than sheep and the ranch, Xabier," Jenny says. "Well, here's your chance."

"I don't want a chance."

"Really?"

Jenny takes my hand. I should pull away, but I don't.

Idetta will be wondering where I've been. What lie will I tell her? I was out looking for a lost lamb? In town buying supplies?

Jenny turns my hand over and traces the tip of her finger along my palm. Her touch flutters like a butterfly over my skin. Back when we dated, she used to pretend she could read the future in the lines of my palm, and in that future we were always together.

"Do you ever think about what might have been, Xabier?"

A thousand bees seem to be buzzing in my head—like the day Jenny left and the buzzing swarmed through me, erasing the future I'd dreamed of and destroying the life I wanted. Still wanted? The smell of her skin, the touch of her hand—no longer separated by years and loss and betrayal—give birth to a deep, throaty longing for the past.

Tires crackle over asphalt. I turn to see Louie's truck coming toward us; the alley is a shortcut from his store to the downtown. I relax. Louie will understand.

Only it isn't Louie behind the steering wheel, but his wife, Pascaline. Her lips draw into a tight line as she drives past.

I pull my hand from Jenny's. "I have to get home."

› › › *opening a door*

Idetta is leaving when I arrive.

She loads the baby into the used Kia we bought last year—the car she hates and says smells like cat piss and is like driving a shoe box.

I hurry over. "Need some help?"

Idetta fastens the baby into his seat. "I can do it on my own."

Haugi curls up on the passenger's side.

"Why you taking the dog?"

"You mean *your* dog?"

I exhale. "Can I ask where you're going?"

"Pascaline's." Idetta throws her friend's name at me like a slap. Pascaline was probably on the phone before I even started my truck, telling Idetta about Jenny and what she thinks she saw.

Idetta gets into the Kia but doesn't turn the ignition. As if waiting for me to say something—to explain what I have done, what I am still doing. But how do I explain to her about Jenny? What she said. Threatened. How do I get her to understand my overriding need to prove Jenny wrong? Because that's what I plan to do. To make sure everyone knows Dad's death was an accident. Nothing more.

I swing close the Kia's door. "When will you be back?"

"I don't know." Idetta's face pinches tight—my words not what she hoped for. "I fed *your aitatxi* breakfast."

"Thanks."

"I didn't do it for you."

I lay my hand on her forearm. "Nothing happened."

Idetta slides her arm out from under my hand. "The same nothing that happened between that girl and your father?"

My faces flushes hot as I stammer, "Wh...what are you talking about?"

"Don't play dumber than you are, Xabier." Idetta starts the car. "Pascaline told me she saw them at Mendia's."

Dad at Louie's store with Jenny? Why didn't Louie let me know?

"Anything you need to tell me, Xabier?"

Her question is like an opening in a fence to be slipped through—my chance to speak the truth and free myself from the secrets weighing me down, the deceptions causing my shoulders to burn, my neck to cramp. And I want to—I do. Only the hope of saving the ranch stops me.

I don't know how—can't even imagine a way to do it. But telling Idetta the truth about Dad and Jenny and the foreclosure will only lead to questions about the accident. Questions I'm not ready to answer.

So instead of the whole truth, I go in for part of it. "I didn't know Jenny and my father were at Mendia's."

"That's all?"

I give a single nod.

"Fine then." Idetta puts the Kia into drive. "Father Kieran said he's stopping by later to check on you—maybe you can give him your confession."

Gravel sprays as she speeds away.

"Idetta wait!" I sprint after the car, wanting to confess the truth and try to explain—even if it's useless, even if I use all the wrong words.

But it's too late.

The Kia accelerates down the road.

When the dust settles, I am alone in a way I have never been. Dad gone, Idetta gone, my son gone, and Aitatxi leaving me second by second.

I open and close my hands. All the things I have tried to hold on to slipping through my fingers. The world pulling them away from me. Even though I know where I stand—in Arizona, on the ranch, outside the barn—I am lost. A cyclone twists through me—life and death, right and wrong, lies and truth. How did I get here? To this moment? And how do I find my way home?

I turn and walk toward the barn.

When I push open the door, sunlight falls over the Farmall. The tractor with its missing tire tilts onto its side; the weathered tire propped up against the barn's wall.

Dad taking off the tire in order to get better access to the tractor's inner mechanisms...wanting to work his hands into its heart...into places previously unreachable...the lug nuts groaning as he loosened them...the cracked rubber reminding him of the day we drove to Kingman to buy the tire...the way it rained the whole way there—turning the gray road black...the steaming coffee we gulped as we chased a rainbow home.

Fresh gravel has been spread over the area around the tractor. Something Louie and Jean must have done. To cover up the blood. A Band-Aid over an unhealed wound.

Txauri scurries past me. With her nose to the ground, the dog begins searching every inch of the barn as if determined to find the man who went in and never came out.

Thin lines of light filter through gaps in the planks of the walls. Overhead there's a new rafter beam. Louie and Jean again. My friends fixing what they could in my life. The unpainted beam is in stark contrast to the rest of the barn's weathered wood. Like a sapling amid a cluster of ancient oaks.

I step farther into the barn.

The come-along winch with its chain and hook are bunched on the ground. The tractor jack used to lift the Farmall off Dad sits near the dark spot where his hand lay.

My hands begin to shake, and it is like I am falling backward into a giant hole whose bottom I may never reach. A sob rips through me—unyielding as a harrow blade. Another begins rising from deep inside me. I wrap my arms around my chest and try to hold in my grief.

Daddy, Daddy, Daddy.

I grab the come-along. Tears blur my vision as I loosen the chain's slack and heave the hooked end of the chain toward the new rafter beam. Dust shoots like smoke from a smoldering fire as the hook and chain fall in a tangled knot at my feet. I slide the back of my forearm across my eyes, straighten out the chain, and throw the hook again; this time it clears the beam.

The hook swings in front of my face.

Txauri comes to stand beside me. The dog whines.

"Quiet, girl."

I take hold of the metal hook and attach it to the front of the tractor and begin cinching up the slack.

As the tractor shudders and slowly rises from the dirt, I get the dizzying feeling I am undoing time, running the clock backward in an attempt to regain what was lost. The exertion of pumping the winch carves into my grief like water into a riverbank. Physical pain flows through me. Fingers aching, forearms cramping. I keep pumping until the tractor rises three feet off the ground—just enough room for a man to slip beneath.

I let go of the winch handles and double over, heart hammering as I gaze up. Even from a distance, I can tell the new beam is nothing like the old. The lines of grain straight and true. No bow to its middle. The wood solid and able to bear the weight.

I drop my eyes to the open space under the tractor. The last spot my father occupied in this world. I get on my knees and slide under the elevated tractor.

The smell of grease and oil swirl as the warmth of the ground seeps through my shirt. I dislodge a pebble pressing into the base of my skull and toss it to the side. Above me hangs the red frame of the Farmall. Light falling into the barn stops at the edge of the tractor. If I reach out a hand, I can touch it.

Txauri comes over to lick dried tears from my face. I push her away. She trots off and out the door, unable to find what she was looking for.

I bump the chassis. The tractor sways from side to side as the chain rattles against the fender.

Oh Dad, did the dirt, the sweat, the heat…the frustration of not being able to fix all the broken things in your life cause you to give in to defeat? Or did you want to fight on—find a way to tell me the truth so we could fix the problem together? Did the beam break before you could slip from beneath the tractor? Or were you waiting for it to snap? Was your irrintzina let loose in defiance of life's adversity? Or were you calling to Mom—letting her know she would no longer be alone?

The cooing of doves floats down from above. The birds jockey for roost along the new beam. Their fluttering gray wings beat the air, and amid them I catch a flash of white.

My heart batters my ribs.

A stupid reaction. The white dove has nothing to do with my father or me or what happened or didn't happen. It is just a bird lacking pigmentation. Yet, I am here, in the barn, the place where Dad last lived, and so is the white dove.

Fuck it.

I slide out from under the Farmall just as the come-along winch snaps—the chain clattering as it unravels.

I roll onto my side as the tractor's axle digs into the ground inches from my skull.

Dust covers me as the doves swoop down from the rafters. The white dove glows within a cloud of gray as the birds fly out the open barn door, right over the head of a pale and wide-eyed Father Kieran who utters, "Holy shit!"

› › › *telling a story*

As I sit with Father Kieran on the porch, both of us still shaken, I think about telling him the story of the lamiak as a way to explain what I was doing in the barn.

But the lamiak story doesn't quite work. The lamiak try to fix things like chairs and lamps, things that can be fixed if the lamiak only knew how. Nothing can *fix* the way my father died.

Flies buzz around us as Father Kieran sips a glass of water. "That was... dangerous."

I swat at a fly. "I know."

Sweat beads along the top of the apaiza's clerical white collar. "What exactly were you trying to accomplish?"

"Not kill myself," I say, and wish I hadn't. Probably not something an apaiza wants to hear.

I think of taking Idetta's advice and giving Father Kieran my confession. Safe in the knowledge of his oath of silence, I could tell him how I was trying to prove my father's death was an accident so whatever Jenny says won't matter and I'll get all the money from the life insurance policy and save the ranch and make Dad proud.

But all those things really come down to one reason. "I want to understand."

"Understand what?"

"What happened the day he died in the barn."

Txauri has resumed her position in the dirt by the open barn door. A gust of wind skitters over the ground and kicks up a flurry; Txauri closes her eyes as it passes over her. Once gone, the dog gets up, shakes off the dust, and slips into the barn.

"So do you?"

"Not yet."

Father Kieran sets his glass of water on the porch. "Saint Augustine said, 'All truth and understanding is a result of a divine light which is God himself.'"

"I have no idea what that means."

He shrugs. "We don't know what we don't know."

"Now that I understand."

We share a brief laugh. When it dies away, the apaiza says, "Back in Ireland, my da was struck by a car while making a delivery—he was a butcher."

"How long?"

"Five years now." Father Kieran presses his hands together. "After it happened, I searched for a long while to understand why that day on that road at that time."

"And?"

"Understanding is like a shadow dancing on the wall." Father Kieran gazes off into space, like he does in church, as if searching for another quote from Saint whoever. "Try and close your hands on that shadow and it slips right through your fingers."

"Who said that?"

Father Kieran's cheeks redden. "Me."

"You should think about using more of your own quotes in the Homily."

"I'll do that," he says with a shy smile.

Txauri pokes her head out of the barn and fixes her gaze on me, as if she has found something inside—*another shadow of understanding dancing on the wall?*

"It took a long time after Da died for me to recognize that you don't have to understand everything that happens in life, Xabier—you just have to find a way to accept it."

"That's what Idetta said."

"Smart woman."

"Amen to that, Father," I say as sunlight hits the barn door's steel hinges, causing them to flare and send flames of reflected light up the walls of the barn.

And I realize both the apaiza and Idetta are right.

Not about the accepting thing—but the understanding.

I don't have to understand everything that happened the day my father died—I just have to make sure no one else does either.

› › › *making a plan*

As I gaze down at the barn through Aitatxi's bedroom window, I roll the lighter over and over in my hand. I picture flames devouring the barn's walls, peeling away the Farmall's red paint and melting the tractor's greasy heart.

Fires happen on ranches. Dried-out hay bales, spilled gasoline, forgotten cans of oil.

Sometimes people raise an eyebrow at the timing of such "accidents"—like when bills are due or after a bad lambing season. On occasion, the insurance company refuses to pay. But there won't be any investigation into this fire because I won't be making a claim.

I chew my lower lip. If I could only have five more minutes with my father. One last conversation. A chance to find different answers to our problems—solutions not ending in fire and death. But would Dad tell me his hard truths? Would I tell him mine? Or would we talk about painting the barn and harvesting alfalfa? Familiar things, easy things.

Suicide. The sharp consonants and bitter vowels leave a metallic sting on my tongue. A foreign word—from a language I don't want to learn or know or understand.

I close my eyes and again see my father's hand reaching out from under the Farmall. I try and replace the image with one of Dad sipping red wine at the dinner table or sitting on the porch talking about the flock or walking through the pasture in the evening. But I can't.

Are my memories of him already fading? Like with Mom and Amatxi?

What shade of brown was my mother's hair? What color were

Amatxi's eyes? Right now, no matter how I concentrate, I can't picture either. The images of the two women who raised me and I still love so much every beat of my heart recalls them have become like photos left on a windowsill, the colors bleached out by the Arizona sun.

I pull from my back pocket the life insurance policy Dad took out on me the day I graduated from the U of A.

Did he get it before he came down to Tucson for the ceremony? Or later? When I told him I was leaving for California?

After graduation, we ate lunch at a Mexican restaurant near campus. Dad talked about putting in a new fence behind the barn and how the porch deck needed replacing. Then, as he started listing the other ranch summer projects he had lined up for us, I blurted out, "Jenny and I are moving to Los Angeles."

I held my breath. Ready for a scowl to appear on my father's face and for him to shake his head and say, *You think that's a smart thing to do?* But instead, he said, "You know, you're the first Etxea to graduate college. Your mother would be proud of you, Xabier—I know I am."

His words knocked the breath out of me.

The next day, I drove to the ranch with everything from my dorm crammed into the bed of my truck. Jenny was set to meet me in LA later in the week. I just needed to grab some clothes from the house and I'd be off.

When I reached the ranch, I stopped on the ridge overlooking the north pasture and gazed down at the flock—glowing like a celestial cloud descended from heaven. Each morning for an hour or so dew covered the sheep's wool so that they radiated with reflected sunlight. The occurrence was both beautiful and fleeting. As the sun rose higher, the dew evaporated and the flock returned to its mundane reality.

A reality I wanted to escape.

The sheep were always there, always needing caring. Part of the ranch's tiny world of repetition—fences broken, repaired, broken again; crops planted, harvested, replanted; breakfast, lunch, dinner; morning, noon, night.

Me, Dad, Aitatxi locked in a never-ending cycle.

But no more. I was free.

Dad pulled up in his truck and came to stand beside me. "Ready to hit the road?"

"More than ready."

"You know I almost moved to California once."

"Why didn't you?"

Dad squatted and pulled up a clump of grass and let the blades fall through his fingers. "The dream of the land stopped me."

I raised an eyebrow. "The dream of the land?"

"Night and day the dream called to me, 'Ferdinand, where do you think you're going? Your dream is here.'"

I dropped my head and dug the toe of my boot into the dirt and attributed my father's sudden poetic outburst to his not wanting me to go.

I touched his shoulder. "I'll miss you too, Dad."

He smiled, stood, and said, "Gotta go—the dream of the land is calling."

Without looking back, he waded into the flock.

I checked the time on my phone. If I left right then, I could be on Sunset Boulevard in time for lunch.

I didn't move.

Jenny would be waiting for me to call and let her know I was on my way.

I didn't dial.

Clouds danced along the horizon—the warmth of the sun spread over my face.

I didn't turn away.

My breaths came and went, each pull of air reaching deeper into me. I was leaving. The wind whistled over the grass. I was going. A humming, low and urgent, rose from the ground and vibrated up through my feet. I wouldn't listen.

I closed my eyes.

But the humming persisted. A familiar melody whose origin escaped me—an old song made suddenly new—swelled inside me as it transformed into the piercing crescendo of an irrintzina, "Ai-ai-ai-ai-ai-ai-ai-yaaaaa!"

I let out a gasp and opened my eyes.

My father stood amid the flock, head thrown back, his irrintzina shooting into the sky, "Ai-ai-ai-ai-ai-ai-ai-yaaaaa!"

And in each rising note of his irrintzina, the land called to me, *Xabier, where do you think you're going? Your dream is here.*

My body shook as something inside me struggled to break free. The past, the present, the future—all flames of the same fire burning in me.

I threw back my head and let loose my irrintzina, "Ai-ai-ai-ai-ai-ai-ai-yaaaaa!"

My irrintzina rose to entwine with my father's, and like the loop of a lasso, our irrintzina encircled us—pulled tight—bound us together.

Me—a pebble dropped into a pool of water, sending ripples out over the land; Dad—the center of a compass whose needle forever pointed home.

When our irrintzina faded, my heart again beat gently, only it beat differently now. I drove to the house, unpacked my truck, and called Jenny.

I jam the insurance policy back into my pocket and go over to stand beside Aitatxi.

He lies on his back in bed, eyes closed, hands folded. I try to get him to eat a piece of sourdough toast. But it's no use; Aitatxi keeps his lips firmly closed and won't even take a sip of water.

I want to force open his eyes, unfold his hands, to shake him and yell, *Get up! There is work to do and life to live!*

But then I wonder if Idetta is right about Aitatxi no longer wanting to be here.

I rub the lighter between my thumb and index finger as I lean over and kiss my aitatxi on the forehead; the warmth on his skin from yesterday is gone.

Aitatxi mumbles, "Osozuriaerrazu—" no longer having the strength to separate his words, consonants and vowels blurring together, forming a new word belonging to the language of death.

› › › *building a fire*

I lock Txauri in the house to keep her safe,

The dog barks in protest—as if she wants to be part of what I am going to do. But this job is mine alone.

I walk over to the barn and prepare to set fire to *understanding*.

With no physical evidence to back her up, Jenny will come off as a gold digger looking to make money off my father's death. Dad's name might get muddied a bit in the process, but better than the alternative.

When I open the barn door, cool air slides over my face and tightens my skin. Everything is so still. So quiet. I half expect Dad to step from the shadows and ask me what I am doing.

What would I tell him? Cleaning up your mess?

Which is now my mess.

I use my foot to form a mound of straw near the door, so if things get out of control I can make a quick exit.

From a stack of cast-off wood, I grab a warped board to break up for kindling. A row of scallop-shaped cuts runs down its length. I press my fingers into the cuts—which belong to me. Aitatxi made me practice on discarded wood boards before allowing me to carve something on my own. The first thing I did carve was a shepherd's crook. I etched a winding vine up the length of the crook and at the tip of the hook shaped a wolf's head. I thought it was so cool. Aitatxi said it was a good beginning—even if the head looked more like it belonged to a cow than a wolf.

I bust up the board and drop the pieces beside the straw. I gather more splintered boards along with a pair of discarded chair legs and a worn tabletop. I pile them near the barn's door. I will feed the fire with wood until the hungry flames grow big enough to devour the barn and all its secrets.

I go in search of gasoline.

At the back of the barn, busted siphon hoses and cracked funnels litter the ground. Why didn't I ever clean up this stuff? Among the discarded junk, I find a half-full container of gas and a few cans of Shell oil—for some reason the only brand Dad ever bought.

Since anything flammable will help, I carry the oil along with the gasoline back to the barn's opening.

I kneel and pull the lighter from my pocket.

Txauri starts barking again. Her barks turn into howls.

I block out the noise and flick on the lighter. The flame dances in my hand. My heart races like when I was a kid, standing on the edge of the hayloft, getting ready to leap into the hay piled on the barn's floor, to fly through the nothingness toward what I hoped would be a soft landing.

I touch the lighter to the straw; it crackles and blackens. I blow on the flame and feed it bits of the board covered in rows of my scallop-shaped cuts. The wood burns orange, then red.

With heat on my face and sweat coating my skin, I put larger pieces of board into the fire—the flames reach chest high.

Time for the oil.

But as I reach for a can, a white dove flutters through the open barn door and lands on the dirt a few feet away. Where did it come from? Through the flames separating us, the bird fixes its dark eyes on me. Why is it here?

You're too late—I've made my decision—I don't need you anymore.

And yet I hold my breath, afraid this might be my last chance for...what? ...forgiveness? Is that what I think the white dove holds? Forgiveness from my father? But shouldn't he be asking forgiveness of me? Or is it something beyond forgiveness I am searching for?

I stretch a hand toward the dove—pain breaks the spell as fire scorches my fingers.

"Fuck!" I yank back my hand.

The dove coos but doesn't fly away.

I scoop up fistfuls of dirt and throw them onto the fire. The flames sputter. Gray smoke turns black.

On hands and knees, I crawl around the dying embers toward the white dove. All my focus on the bird—willing it to stay—determined not to let this shadow of understanding slip through my hands.

When I am within arm's reach, I get ready to lunge, but before I can, a net drops over the dove.

"Gotcha." A gray-haired man wearing red suspenders scoops up the bird.

I scramble to my feet. "What are you doing?"

The man glances past me at the remains of the fire. "Didn't your wife tell you?"

I stomp out the smoldering flames. "Tell me what?"

"One of my doves got out." The man rubs the cooing bird against his cheek. "Dr. Berria said he saw a white dove when he was out here. Gave me your number. I called and talked to your wife. She said I could come over and take a look."

"The white dove belongs to you?"

"A hobby of mine." The man's attention shifts to the cans of oil and container of gas.

I snatch up the lighter from the dirt. "You keep doves?"

"White doves." He lodges the net under his arm. "But this bad boy literally flew the coop. I've been searching for days. He's lucky I found him. White doves don't survive long in the world—too conspicuous—make easy targets for predators."

I brush off my pants and follow the man out of the barn to where his blue van sits parked by the porch.

Txauri still barks. The man's arrival probably the reason she started.

The old man opens the van's back doors to reveal cages full of white doves. He puts my white dove into an empty cage, then shuts the van's doors.

The man looks back toward the barn. "Everything okay here?"

"Just cleaning things up is all."

"Be careful—fires have a way of getting out of control." The man gives his red suspenders a flick as he climbs in and starts the engine. "Thanks again for my bird."

The dust from the departing van settles over me. My white dove one of many. Nothing mystical or magical about the bird. No redemption or understanding dripping off its white wings. The dove nothing but a pet, kept in a cage—an old man's hobby.

I stumble to my truck, climb in, and drive.

> > > *running in place*

I drive into Urepel and turn down Izara Street.

A boy runs in front of my truck. I slam the brakes, honk the horn. But the boy doesn't even look back as he sprints away, and for a moment, I run with him. Because I am him—thirteen years ago. A boy causing near traffic accidents on a daily basis. Always running to the library, the drugstore, the baseball diamond. Life packed with places to go and me always in a hurry to get there—screeching brakes and honking horns trailing like smoke in my wake.

The boy cuts down the alley behind Bide Drugstore and disappears.

I take my foot off the brake and turn into Mendia's Feed and Tackle.

The parking lot is full of trucks belonging to ranchers stocking up on supplies. Like me, once the lambs start to drop, there will be no time to do anything but protect their flocks.

I pull into an open space next to Idetta's Kia.

Inside Mendia's, Pete Espil examines grades of fence wire, Henri Etxemendi fills a paper bag with corn feed, Michael Itcaina rolls a spare tire toward the exit.

I cut down Aisle 4 toward the back of the store where a blue door wedged between stacks of tractor tires marks the entrance to Louie and Pascaline's home—intimately connecting their private and work lives.

"She's not here." Louie stands atop a ladder restocking a shelf with boxes of shotgun casings.

"Her Kia's out front."

"Broke down." Louie pushes the last of the boxes onto the shelf. "Jean's going to take a look at it."

"Where is she?"

"Pascaline drove her and the baby home to get some things."

"What things?"

"Ask your wife." Louie descends the ladder, stopping a couple of rungs from the bottom to shake his head. "Why didn't you just tell Idetta you were going to see Jenny?"

"Why didn't you tell me Jenny was here with my dad?"

The question seems to surprise Louie. Though I'm not sure why. He knows how Pascaline likes to talk.

"It wasn't really about why, Xabier." Louie gets off the ladder. "More like how."

"How?"

"How to tell my best friend his father is seeing his ex-fiancée."

"You should have found a way."

"You're right." Louie averts his eyes, traces his fingers along a shelf crammed with every size nut and bolt imaginable. "I'm sorry."

The muscles of Louie's jaw clench and unclench, as if he's trying to chew up and swallow words he doesn't want to say.

I set my jaw. "Is there something more you're sorry for?"

Louie opens his mouth, but no words come out.

"When did my father come in with Jenny?"

"You got to understand, Xabier." Louie starts talking fast, words rushing out like water from a ruptured pipe. "Your dad had been running up a pretty big bill and I didn't know—"

—"When?"

"Last Saturday."

I lean closer. "What did he come in for?"

"His credit was overextended and Pascaline was on me about it and I told him if he could just pay a little—"

—I grab the front of Louie's shirt. "What did he want?"

"A tractor jack."

I let go of Louie and stagger backward as if punched in the face.

"He never said what he needed it for. If he'd told—I'm so sorry, Xabier."

At Louie's apology, hot anger surges through me. I swing my arm along the nearest shelf, sending nuts and bolts clattering over the tile floor.

"Being *sorry* doesn't bring him back!"

Patrons stop and turn to see what's going on.

I want to yell at them to mind their business, but then a strange lightness fills my body and my shoulders relax as the tension leaves my neck. My father came to buy a jack. He planned on using it to remove the Farmall's tire so he could fix the tractor. He wanted to do it the right way. But couldn't. Which proves what happened in the barn *was* an accident.

The truth of Louie's words makes Jenny's words a lie.

› › › *learning to dance*

On the drive to the ranch, my thoughts ricochet between what Louie said and what I am going to tell Idetta.

Dad at Mendia's Feed and Tackle. Trying to buy a tractor jack. Over-extended credit.

I should call Idetta and set the groundwork for my apology. Tell her how I just forgot to mention my meeting up with Jenny. That's all. Slipped my mind. Didn't do it on purpose.

Why would Dad take Jenny to Louie's store? Did he know Louie wouldn't tell me? Or didn't he care? Not trying to hide their relationship? Only why then didn't he tell me?

What if Idetta and the baby are gone when I get home? She wouldn't leave. Not over one little lie—which wasn't even really a lie but just an omission. Would she?

Only I didn't think my father would be with my ex. And I didn't think Jenny would try and blackmail me. Or that Louie would keep Dad's debt a secret.

Damn it. So many people have done so many things I didn't think they would—could Idetta be one more?

When I turn into the ranch yard, relief tingles over my skin at the sight of my wife sitting on the front porch steps.

Just how much of the truth do I need to tell her?

Now is probably not the best time to start bulldozing away at the mountain of other things I've not shared with her. All the stuff about the foreclosure and the life insurance policy can come out later. Best to start slowly—with Jenny. Because confessing everything at once will get her back on the phone to Pascaline. Better to wait until everything settles down before coming totally clean. Only what if I never get that chance?

I go and sit beside Idetta on the porch steps.

The chickens cluck and the dogs bark and the sheep baaa and the sun moves toward a horizon bringing me one day closer to…what? Losing my wife? Saving the ranch?

"I should have never gone to see her."

Idetta corrects me. "You should have never gone to see her without telling me."

"It was just about my father." I hold a hand out to her, palm up. "That's the only reason I met with her—I swear."

Idetta wearily shakes her head before placing her hand into mine. "Oh, my Xabier, you are lucky I know you."

I squeeze Idetta's hand. "Then you understand?"

"About you lying about going to see your ex-fiancée?" Idetta slaps my shoulder. "Of course not."

"But you know me?"

"Just because I know you doesn't mean I understand everything you do."

"How can you know somebody without understanding what they do?"

"Ha, do you know me?"

"C'mon Idetta, this isn't—"

—"Did you know I wanted to be a dancer."

"You were a dancer."

"Not a Basque folk dancer, I did that to please my ama." Idetta stands. "I wanted to go to New York and dance at the Met and be a ballerina."

"A ballerina?"

"That's right." Idetta throws a heavy leg over the porch railing. "I practiced for hours in the barn, just me and the cows." With a clumsy elegance I didn't know she possessed, my wife stretches her arm in a perfect arch over her head. "I'd pretend the bits of straw floating through the air were snowflakes and I the fairy queen."

Idetta hums a tune as she does half a pirouette, loses her balance, and with a laugh grabs on to the post to keep from falling.

Stunned, and a little in awe, I shrug. "I didn't know."

She plops back down next to me. "So you understand my practicing alone in the barn to be a ballerina?"

Idetta's no-nonsense approach to life doesn't fit neatly with the idea of her being a ballerina fairy queen. In fact, try as I may, I can't picture Idetta in a pink tutu pirouetting across a stage. I also can't think how telling her that is in any way a good idea. So instead I say, "Why didn't you go to New York?"

Idetta brushes a hand through her hair. "I don't have the bones of a ballerina."

I put a hand on her leg. "You have beautiful bones."

"True—just not beautiful ballerina bones." Idetta places her hand over mine. "The point is you knowing I wanted to be a ballerina doesn't mean you understand why."

"You could explain it to me."

Idetta shakes her head. "A million words would not be enough to explain the joy of getting on point for an audience of mooing cows. Yet you know me better than anyone in the world."

"Obviously not as well as I thought."

"That keeps things interesting." Idetta kisses my cheek. "But Xabier, you ever go see that Jenny girl again without tell me, and you'll be eating your own mountain oysters for Sunday dinner."

"Got it."

Idetta gets to her feet. "I'm going to check on the baby."

The kitchen door bangs shut. I stretch my arms up over my head and let out a whistling breath. Even though I don't quite get or buy into Idetta's knowing-and-understanding theory, at least the whole meeting-up-with-Jenny thing is settled.

Now if I could just get the stuff Louie kicked up settled as well.

In the distance, clouds are building, one on top of the other, like a flock of sheep rushing to get through a narrow gate. Too early for a monsoon. The storms still months away. These clouds only a mirage, destined to flatten out and dissipate.

I get to my feet and take out my cell phone. I call Fred and tell him I want an investigation into my father's death.

> > > *singing a song*

Bolts of lightning shatter the night. The storm I didn't think would come has arrived.

"His appetite is better." Idetta spoons soup into Aitatxi's mouth. She lays the back of her hand against his forehead. "More warmth to his skin."

I press my hand against Aitatxi's bedroom window; the glass vibrates with rolling thunder. Did I make a mistake in calling Fred? Betting the future of the ranch on my father trying to buy a tractor jack? Will it be proof enough to stop Jenny?

In hastily taken snapshots, the jagged tendrils of lightning momentarily illuminate the flock, the fences, the desert, the barn. I grab hold of the images and wedge them into my memory. Photos in an album to be brought out when the family gathers to reminisce about what once was and is no more?

Fred is coming out in the morning—too late to stop it now. But what if an investigation reveals things I didn't foresee?

Later tonight I should tell Idetta more of the truth—let her know what is coming. I'll do it, while we lay in bed, tangled in sheets. She will understand. She has to.

Aitatxi mumbles, "Maitea gatik pasa nintzazke gauak eta egunak."

Idetta sings back, "Gauak eta egunak, desertu eta oihanak."

I frown. "You don't speak Euskara."

"No, but I know the lyrics to 'Uso Zuria, Errazu.'" Idetta sets aside the bowl of soup. "We danced to the song in Idaho."

"That's what he's been saying?"

Idetta wipes a napkin over Aitatxi's lips. "Not saying—singing."

"But he only ever sings the beginning."

"Not anymore." Idetta strokes Aitatxi's cheek. "For my loved ones I would pass nights and days; nights and days, deserts and woods."

I know those words—*nights and days—deserts and woods*—but can't place how.

Down the hall, the baby starts to cry.

"Time for someone else to eat." Idetta gets to her feet. "You coming?"

"In a minute."

I go and sit by Aitatxi and gently touch his forehead—he does feel warmer.

"'Uso Zuria, Errazu'—so that's what you've been singing all this time." I fold the rose-covered quilt in around his body. "But why? Why the rest of the song now?"

I don't expect Aitatxi's eyes to pop open and for him to explain the reasoning of his feverish brain. But I do get a certain comfort from his words and the dove at the funeral being connected. Maybe not in the way I hoped—some grand sign from my father to help me derive meaning from his death. Still, amid all the chaos, there's a peacefulness to Aitatxi singing about a simple white dove.

Aitatxi's lips move as he sings, "Maitea gatik..."

"For my loved ones," I say back to him and smile—because for the first time since Dad's death, we understand each other.

Outside, the storm has moved away, fading into the distance. The thunder now nothing but falling pebbles; the lightning no more than sparks. This day finally over. Tomorrow will bring more challenges and struggles, but then that is part of life—or at least my life. But I'm too tired to think of that now.

I turn off the bedside light and walk to the window. Then, as I start to pull closed the curtains for the night, the barn bursts into flame.

My breath catches in my chest at the suddenness of the attack.

Because that's what it feels like. An attack. Fire shoots up through the barn's roof. The heat of the flames moves through the glass and over my face. Electricity pulses along my skin. My eyes burn.

I can't look away.

The cans of the gas; the dry wood. Combusting? The investigation; the barn burning. I didn't do it. Nowhere near the barn when the fire started. Idetta knows. No matter what the man with the white doves saw. The fire—the flames—no evidence better than any.

The rising flames urge on my pounding heart as a horrible elation fills my chest at the destruction before me.

I whisper, "Burn, burn, burn."

Then I spot Idetta.

She dashes from the porch and across the open area toward the barn.

I slam the palms of my hands against the warm glass of the window. "No—stop!"

But my words burn away into nothingness as my wife runs straight into the flames.

I take the stairs two at a time.

Idetta in the barn—the barn burning.

I can't get my legs to go fast enough—like I'm moving through a flooded field, every step fighting against the water.

The baby with Idetta?

No time to go upstairs and check.

I bust through the kitchen, knocking over the table, glass shatters. I yank open the door. A wave of heat presses against me—tries to drive me back. I shield my face with my arms and sprint toward the barn.

Haugi and Txauri howl. The fire howls. The world howls.

I stumble. Regain my balance. Stagger forward. The barn door thrown open. Inside nothing but flames. Smoke burns my eyes; tears blur my vision. I lower my shoulder and plunge into the fire.

Heat—intense, painful—sears into my brain.

"Idetta!" My throat dry, cracking. "Idetta!"

I am spinning, spinning, spinning. Caught up in a dust devil. Rising into the sky.

"Idetta! Idetta! Idetta!"

Trapped inside a cloud. Smoke everywhere. I gulp for air, but there is none left.

A final sob of defeat rises in my chest as I drop to my knees and there find—lying on the ground, huddled beneath the wall of smoke—my Idetta.

I crawl to her. Grab onto her arm; her skin like embers beneath my fingers. Inch by inch I drag her over the dirt toward the barn's entrance. A thunderous crack overhead. The new beam shatters and crashes down on the Farmall.

Then somehow I am outside. Warm night air like ice on my skin. Idetta's lips moving, forming words I cannot hear.

Lifting her in my arms, I carry her limp body to the porch. I stretch her out onto the wooden planks. Smoke rises from her dress, her hair, her skin.

She coughs. Waves a hand in front of her face. "Xabier?"

"I am here—my love, my love, my love."

I kiss and kiss and kiss every inch of my wife's face, the bitter taste of smoke and ash on my lips, my tongue, in my throat.

Idetta pushes me away. "Water."

I rush inside and get a glass of water. When I step back onto the porch, Idetta is sitting up, leaning against the porch railing, Haugi and Txauri's heads in her lap.

I hand Idetta the glass of water; she gulps it down.

"That was crazy." I brush singed hair from her face. "You could have been killed."

"Someone was in the barn."

"What? No, no one was in there." I shake my head. "Just you."

The barn's roof collapses, sending a plume of fire straight into the night. Embers shoot like tiny stars through the air and land on the wooden porch.

I stomp the embers out. "Take the baby and go into the pasture."

"What about Aitatxi?"

"I'll get him."

As Idetta rushes into the house, I crank on the hose—wash down the porch—spray water over the roof. The horses scream. I drop the hose and run around to the side of the barn. Wild with fear—eyes glistening with flames—the horses are a dance of shadow and light. I yank open the corral gate—they gallop away.

I turn to my truck. The door handle is blistering to the touch. I pull off my shirt, wrap my hand in the cloth, and pull open the door. I slip the truck into neutral and push it away from the barn—doubling over with the effort.

The walls of the barn fold in, igniting a stack of haybales. There is nothing I can do. The fire too big—too powerful for me alone. The flames illuminate the ranch house like the light of a noon-day sun.

Aitatxi.

I start toward the house. But before I take three steps, the sky opens up and rain thunders down.

The retreating storm has circled back.

I open my mouth and let the rain pour into me.

› › › *starting a journey*

"Her burns should be worse." Dr. Berria stands with me outside the bedroom door.

"Then she's okay, right?"

"There's no sign of lung damage." He holds his stethoscope in his hand. "I don't understand how."

I press my fingers to the exposed skin of my arm; it is red and tender to the touch, but no blistering. Like I spent a day outside, got a bad sunburn but nothing more.

"Your wife got lucky—you both did." Dr. Berria shakes his head. "How's your aitatxi doing?"

"I don't think he even knows there was a fire."

"Don't bet on that." Dr. Berria nods knowingly. "I have a hunch your aitatxi is more here than you think and just waiting."

"Waiting for what?"

"Only he knows that." Dr. Berria starts toward Aitatxi's room. "I'm going take a peek in on him."

As Dr. Berria heads down the hall, I get the feeling whatever Aitatxi's been waiting for has arrived. The world shifting. On the verge of losing it all, suddenly everything given back. All because of a fire I am innocent of starting.

While Dr. Berria checks over Aitatxi, I call Fred and let him know what happened.

Tomorrow, we'll meet. Together we will walk through the ashes of the barn; I will ask for an advance on my father's life insurance payout and use the money to hire someone to help me with the lambing.

I let out a deep breath. Soon all of this will be behind me. I slip into the bedroom to check on Idetta and the baby.

"How you doing?"

Idetta takes a lock of her scorched hair. "I'm going to have to cut this all off."

I flop on the bed next to her. "I like short hair."

"That's because it's not your hair."

I lay my hand on the baby's chest, tiny heartbeats tap against my palm. "Did he sleep through everything?"

"He's a good sleeper."

I kiss the top of my son's head.

There's a soft knocking on the door; Dr. Berria pokes his head in. "I'll be going."

I get up from the bed. "How's Aitatxi?"

"The same."

"Still waiting?"

"Uh, huh." Dr. Berria fiddles with the doorknob as if he is going to say something more, but doesn't.

Idetta resettles herself in the bed. "Thank you for coming."

"Of course, you're like family." Dr. Berria stands up straighter. "Remember—apply the ointment twice a day and call me if either of you have any trouble breathing."

"We'll be fine," Idetta says.

"Lucky." He smiles. "Really lucky."

I walk Dr. Berria out to his car.

The rain has stopped. Not even smoke now. As if the fire happened years ago. Only the smell lingers. How many days will it hang in the air?

"You're right, Dr. Berria, we were lucky."

"Let's just hope that luck holds." Dr. Berria places his medicine bag in the car. "Because your aitatxi can't wait much longer."

"You said he was the same?"

"You're a rancher, Xabier; you know nothing in nature stays the same for long." Dr. Berria places a hand on my shoulder. "Life either changes for the better or . . . well, there comes a time when you need to stop waiting."

As Dr. Berria drives away, his tires splash through the puddles dotting the area between the house and barn, shattering reflected stars and muddying the night.

I walk over to where the barn stood. A dark smudge on the ground. No walls, no roof. A hole cut into the night. An empty space needing filling.

What if the beam had fallen on Idetta?

What if I didn't find her in time?

What if we both died in the fire?

I force myself to turn away—the remnants of the barn contain too many *what ifs* for a lucky night to hold.

My phone dings. Jenny's name appears: *I heard there was a fire—you okay?*

No secrets in a small town.

I fight the urge to throw down my phone and grind it into pieces under my heel. Then I recall Dr. Berria's words, "There comes a time when you need to stop waiting."

So instead of deleting Jenny's text, I text her back: *It's over—leave me and my family alone.*

I get an immediate response: *We need to talk.*

I turn off the power to my phone and jam it into my pocket.

SATURDAY—THE PASCHAL VIGIL

For where your treasure is,
there will your heart be also.

MATTHEW 6:21

›› finding a heart

Before getting dressed in the morning, I rub the ointment Dr. Berria left over my arms and face. Heat radiates from my skin as if I am still in the barn, lost and surrounded by flames.

I pull on my clothes and then, before leaving the bedroom, wiggle the baby's foot and run my fingers over Idetta's seared hair. *This is mine, this is mine—I will hold tight.*

I check on Aitatxi. His eyes flutter beneath closed lids. What does he see? Who is he remembering?

From the doorway, I whisper, "Time to stop waiting, Aitatxi."

Downstairs in the kitchen, I pick up the table I knocked over last night. Morning light falls into the kitchen, trickles over the counters, spills onto the floor littered with the shards of Ama's ceramic Gateau Basque bowl.

I sweep up the broken pieces and pour them into the trash.

Then I go into the living room, still more dark than light. Sunlight has not yet reached the room. I move through shadows, touch the mantel I carved, press my hand to the chair Idetta always sits in, trace my fingers over the coffee table littered with home renovation magazines—things I pass daily but never really notice, until now. The fire has transformed each into something precious and rare.

Outside on the porch, I drink my coffee.

Despite the burned ground and air tinged with smoke, there's an underlying freshness to the day—like a field cleared for new planting. To the east sits a distant mountain capped with the remnant of winter snow. A mountain previously hidden by the barn, now made visible by the fire.

Using my phone, I type in an ad for a ranch hand, *Experience with sheep a plus.* I post it on the local community website.

Then I get to work.

I round up the horses and put them in the north pasture. They can stay there until I have time to rebuild the corral. Next I go load up Haugi and Txauri; without hesitation, both dogs jump into the bed of my truck, tails wagging, whining with anticipation. Now that the barn is gone, my father's hold on Txauri is gone.

In the east pasture, the dogs find four newborn lambs nestled in the grass. This marks the official start of the lambing season. Which means coyotes.

In the shade of the same oak tree I stood beneath with Fred just three days ago, I pick up a branch from the ground, pull out my pocket knife, and absently start to carve. If all the other ranchers' flocks drop at the same time as mine, finding help could be difficult. I might have to expand my search to Kingman. Maybe even Phoenix.

For now, I can leave the dogs to watch over the flock. At least during the day. But what about tonight? And all the nights to follow?

By the time I decide to post another ad in both Kingman and Phoenix, I have found the isiliko behotza of the wood—a star with points as sharp as needle tips.

When I get back to the ranch house, Idetta is frying eggs in the kitchen while my son bangs his spoon on his plate. Nice, normal, everyday chaos.

I hold the tiny star I carved in front of Idetta's face. "Make a wish?"

"Oh, my Xabier," Idetta says, "making a wish today would be greedy."

I place the star on the windowsill. "I feel greedy."

The eggs sizzle and pop in the skillet as I take a seat at the table and tap a finger on my son's plate in time with his banging spoon. "Uso zuria errazu…"

Idetta slides a plate of eggs in front of me. "No singing at the table."

"But we live for music."

"Not while we're eating." She takes a bit of egg from my plate and blows on it before giving it to the baby. "After breakfast, I'm going to Pascaline's so she can cut my hair."

"What did she say about the fire?"

"Same as Dr. Berria—that we were lucky."

"I like being lucky."

"If you let me use the truck to go to Pascaline's, you might get lucky later."

"Oh baby, you hear the way your mama talks?" I give my son a bit of egg. "Always taking advantage of me."

Idetta playfully slaps me on the back.

"Go ahead and take the truck." I shovel eggs into my mouth. "I have to stick around until Fred shows up."

Idetta wipes the baby's mouth with the edge of her dress. "Maybe we'll get enough from the fire insurance for a new kitchen."

"I thought you weren't making wishes today."

"Not a wish—a necessity." Idetta places her hand on my arm. "Xabier, thank you."

"For what?"

"Saving me."

"C'mon, Idetta, you—"

—"I never should have gone into the barn." Idetta tightens her grip on my arm. "But I swear I saw somebody in there."

Before I can assure her the barn was empty, there's a knock on the door.

Jean pops his head in. "Uh, did you guys know your barn is gone?"

"You hear that Idetta?" I raise my hands in mock surprise. "We've gone and lost another barn."

"Ha ha." Idetta moves back over to the stove. "You want breakfast, Jean? I've got plenty of eggs."

"Maria made waffles."

Idetta smiles. "Show-off."

"I fixed the Kia," Jean says.

"That's a shame," Idetta sits down beside the baby. "I'm still using the truck."

"It's all yours," I say.

Jeans hangs in the doorway. "Hey Xabier, can I talk to you outside?"

Idetta raises an eyebrow. "Man secrets?"

"The best kind." I follow Jean onto the porch. "What's up?"

"I saw your ad." Jean shifts his weight from one leg to the other. "If you're still looking for help, I'll take the job."

"What about your flock?"

"Maria's brothers are visiting from Reno." Jean licks his lips. "They're staying with us for a while and can take care of the flock."

"But why—"

—"I need money, Xabier." Jean drops his head. "Things haven't been going so great...and...well...I'm behind on a lot of bills."

I want to say, *Why didn't you tell me?* But the words get stuck in my throat—tangled up with all the things I haven't told him.

"I'm just glad my aita's not here to see how I screwed things up."

"Your dad was always proud of you."

Jean kicks the porch post. "Hell, maybe I'm just a lousy sheep rancher."

I've known Jean since before I knew anything, always there, always part of my life, but I've never seen him like this, nervous and embarrassed and defeated.

I clear my throat. "Haugi and Txauri are out in the east pasture—I'll give you a ride."

"I can walk."

"But—"

—"Go finish your breakfast." Jean extends his hand to me. "Thanks, Xabier."

"Of course." I awkwardly shake his hand, not as a friend but a boss.

› › › *turning a page*

After Idetta leaves for Pascaline's, I wander over to where the barn stood.

In the daylight I can see that even though flames consumed the entire outside of the barn, inside some things remain. The husk of the tractor rises like a dark larva emerging from the ground; melted wires knot into metal nests; a harrow's charred teeth form a broken grin.

When my phone dings, I expect it to be Jenny and am already preparing an expletive-filled response—but the text is from Louie.

Daaaaaamn—fire—all good?

I hesitate with my fingers over the keypad.

Louie didn't tell me about Dad's debt. Or his trying to buy a tractor jack. Or Jenny.

I picture Louie standing in his store, next to a shelf of spare parts, waiting for my response to his *all good?*—while Jean stands in a field surrounded by my sheep when he ought to be tending his own flock—and me standing amid the remains of a fire I didn't start but wanted to. And even though nothing survived the fire unscathed, things did survive. Maybe not exactly how I remember them. But still recognizable.

I text back: *All good.*

The moment I hit Send, Louie replies: *Beer later.*

I text: *Many.*

I put the phone in my pocket and continue working my way through the rubble of the fire. Fred should be here any minute. I use the tip of my boot to flip over a plow disk. Blackened cans. Broken glass. The charred tip of a board with three scallop marks cut into it.

Tires crack and pop over the gravel behind me. I turn to greet Fred, but instead find Jenny climbing out of her red car.

"You planned this, didn't you, Xabier?"

I brush ashes from my pants. "Sorry to disappoint you."

As Jenny walks over, she says, "You're telling me you had nothing to do with the barn burning down?"

"Nope."

She folds her arms across her chest. "No way this just *happened* all by itself."

"I like to call it fate."

"Call it whatever you want—it doesn't change anything."

"Kind of does." I pick up a stick from the ground. "That and the fact you were at Mendia's with my father."

"What?"

"The day before his accident." I snap the stick in two. "When he tried to buy a tractor jack."

"That's what Ferdinand was doing?"

"Like you didn't know."

"He and Louie went off and talked alone." Jenny smooths her hair. "I stayed by the entrance with Pascaline glaring daggers at me."

"So my dad never said anything about a tractor jack?"

"Nothing."

"Huh, and here I thought you and him talked about everything."

"I swear, Xabier, he didn't tell me."

"I don't believe you."

"It's the truth." She leans toward me, her face inches from mine. "Everything I told you about Ferdinand is true."

"Then I guess it's your word against mine." I toss the broken parts of the stick into the dirt. "And who is going to believe the girl who was screwing her ex-fiancé's father for money?"

The force of the slap across my face jerks my head to the side. Blood spurts from my lip.

"You don't know anything about what Ferdinand and I had."
Her voice shakes. "The things we shared."

I lick blood off my lips. "Then show me."

"How can—"

—"You told me how much you and Dad texted." I spit the
blood on the ground. "Show me his words to you."

"I...I deleted them."

"Of course you did."

"I didn't know I needed to save them." Jenny touches her finger
to her lips. "That he would be gone."

"But he is." With the back of my hand, I wipe away the remain-
ing blood on my mouth. "And now I want you gone."

"Gone?" Her eyes tear up. "Where will I go?"

"I don't care."

"But he promised."

"Promises are made to be broken," I tell her. "You know that
better than anyone."

She squints at me like I'm far off in the distance and not standing right in front of her. "I was wrong about you, Xabier—you
are nothing like your father."

"Go away, Jenny, and don't ever come back."

She stumbles as if shoved. "But I'm lost."

"Go and be lost somewhere else."

My words cut the legs out from under her. Jenny falls to her
knees in the ashes. "I can't do it."

I don't ask her what "it" is. Instead, I turn away. And when
I do, I spot Aitatxi, standing framed in his bedroom window,
watching.

› › › *reading the past*

When I get up to Aitatxi's room, he's lying in bed, eyes closed, quilt pulled tight around his neck. The features of his face sharp as cut stone—wiped clean of emotion.

I move to the window where he stood only moments before. Jenny's red car speeds away. No trail of dust shadows her departure; the rain from last night still holding the earth tight.

When I turn away from the window, I find Aitatxi's hands clutching the top of the quilt—like he is clinging to the edge of cliff, holding on with all his strength to keep from falling into the nothingness below. I want to explain to him the *why* and *how* of what he saw. Get him to understand I did what I had to. But a cloudiness fills my head and obscures the words I need to justify my actions.

Even if I said all the right words, would Aitatxi's version of justice match up with mine? Or would he simply shake his head and tell me another story about the Mamu—like he did the night before I left for college.

"Remember, Xabier, Mamu, he always watching—always there," Aitatxi said from where he stood in my bedroom doorway as I packed.

I laughed at his bringing up the Mamu. "That's creepy and illegal."

"Mamu, he know the right from the wrong."

Didn't Aitatxi realize I was eighteen? The creature who haunted my dreams as a boy no longer held any power over me.

"Sorry, Aitatxi, but they don't allow Mamus at college."

"There only one Mamu, and he everywhere."

"You mean like God?"

"Mamu, he no is God." Aitatxi crossed himself. "Mamu, he here before there a God."

"That doesn't even make sense."

"Mamu is Mamu."

I sighed. Was Aitatxi afraid I'd run wild at the U of A without him and Dad to guide me? Or was he just sad to see me leaving home?

"Don't worry, Aitatxi, I promise I'll be good." I shut my suitcase. "I'll see you at Christmas break."

Aitatxi nodded. "I wait for you."

I step away from the window and go to the side of Aitatxi's bed and instead of explaining what I did and why, I say, "I'm sorry, Aitatxi, but I can't wait for you anymore."

Aitatxi releases his hold on the quilt and softly sings, "For my loved ones I would pass nights and days. Nights and days, deserts and woods."

The words ripple through me like icy water, pulling me down, and swirling me back as I finally remember where I first saw them: my father's room—the words he wrote on a sheet of paper the week before he died.

I rush out of the room and go down the hallway to his son's.

When I open the door, a lone sliver of light falls between the drawn curtains to cut across the floor and bisect my body. From the dresser's top drawer, I take out the copy of *In a Hundred Graves* and slide the folded sheet of paper from between the book's pages.

I yank open the curtains. Light covers me as I sit on my father's bed and again read what he wrote:

For my loved ones I would pass nights and days;
Nights and days, deserts and woods.

Why did he write these lyrics? Who were they for? Did he leave them for me to find? To tell me...show me...what?

I crumple the paper in my hand. More things I will never know.

Out the window, Jean moves through the flock. From this distance, he is a faceless shepherd. He could be anyone. Could be me.

Did my father sit here and watch as I tended the flock? Imagine that I could be him? And he could be me?

Me—him—us.

I think about the day I found Dad sitting on the edge of his bed, looking so much like Aitatxi. If Idetta walked in the room right now, would she mistake me for Dad? Or was Jenny right when she said, *You are nothing like your father.*

My phone dings.

Fred telling me he is running late.

I delete his text.

Then I scroll down and start deleting every text from Jenny. The way she says she deleted all of Dad's.

But did he delete hers?

My fingers stop. My head jerks around toward the Instant Pot box by the door, where my father's phone sits atop his other personal belongings.

I go to the box, take out my father's phone, and plug it into the power cord by the nightstand. It beeps to life.

Dad never set a password even though I told him he should. To keep his texts safe.

"Safe from who?" he asked.

Never imagining the answer was me.

› › › *texting a friend*

4/10

FERDINAND: I fear I have lost my arima. [Text unsent]

4/9

FERDINAND: Ever wish you could just start over?
JENNY: Ferdinand, you need to talk to xabier
FERDINAND: It's too late for talking.
JENNY: No its not
FERDINAND: I don't know what to say.
JENNY: I know xabier—he will understand
FERDINAND: I will think about it.

4/8

FERDINAND: Do you miss California?
JENNY: I miss what i thought cali could have been——or was supposed to be—which is different than missing IT—only im not sure how—sorry—long day.

4/5

FERDINAND: No coffee today.
JENNY: Whats up
FERDINAND: Work.

4/3

JENNY: How did meeting with fred go
FERDINAND: He wants to buy the ranch.
JENNY: Thats good—right
FERDINAND: I can't do it.

JENNY: Why not
FERDINAND: I can't.
JENNY: ???
FERDINAND: I can't.

3/29
FERDINAND: I found a pair of white pelicans nestled in the north
   pasture this morning.
JENNY: Never seen a white pelican
FERDINAND: Must have flown up from the Gulf.
JENNY: Mexico?
FERDINAND: Sending you a picture.
JENNY: Are they lost
FERDINAND: Maybe just taking a vacation.
JENNY: lol
FERDINAND: I am sure they will find their way home.
JENNY: I like that
FERDINAND: It's a good day.
JENNY: You deserve a good day ☺

3/22
JENNY: Wish you could have stayed longer
FERDINAND: Me too.
JENNY: What are we doing
FERDINAND: Just trying to be happy.
JENNY: You make me happy
FERDINAND: Mil esker.

3/16
JENNY: You never finished the story about naming xabier
FERDINAND: Noel wanted to name him after me. I wanted that
   too.
JENNY: Then why didnt you
FERDINAND: I held him.

JENNY: ???
FERDINAND: He was so perfect.
JENNY: So what was the problem
FERDINAND: Ferdinand was too small a name for him.
JENNY: I dont understand
FERDINAND: My son needed a name as big as the sky.
JENNY: Basque men are strange ☺
FERDINAND: That's what Noel said;-)

3/15

JENNY: Million escars—thanks for helping me put together my
bed today
FERDINAND: It was my pleasure.
JENNY: Mine too ☺

3/8

JENNY: Thanks for coffee, Mr. Etxea—sorry i talked so much
about xabier today
FERDINAND: Sorry I talked so much about my wife, Noel.
JENNY: Glad you did—whats that air-ama thing again
FERDINAND: Arima is soul. And please call me, Ferdinand.
JENNY: Cool—see ya next Tuesday, Ferdinand ☺

3/5

JENNY: Hey—can I call you—need to talk
FERDINAND: Of course.

3/1

FERDINAND: Mil esker—thank you.
JENNY: For what—you buying me coffee ☺ thank you

2/28

FERDINAND: Would you like to have a cup of coffee?
JENNY: ☺.

What is most telling about the texts between my father and Jenny are the things left out. The thoughts and actions and feeling leading to a few typed words. Things I can't know. Those, like the unseen tunnels of a prairie dog stretching beneath the earth, remain hidden. A tiny dash, a smiley face—nothing more than a hole marking the entrance to a hidden world.

Arima.

Amatxi told me the word means hope.

But Dad told Jenny it means soul.

Did Amatxi lie to me?

That day in the kitchen, with the light falling through the window, and Amatxi gazing out over the land and seeing what? The flock? Aitatxi working? The setting sun? Something there, beyond the glass, giving her hope? Was it white? And flying up into the sky?

If arima meant hope to Amatxi, did soul come to mean ranch to my father?

I fear I have lost my arima.

I press Dad's phone between the palms of my hands. I taught him how to text, and he texted Jenny about coffee and a bed, my name and white pelicans, Mom and arima.

Only Jenny deleted all Dad's texts.

Because her texts to my father were no more than casual exchanges? Words typed and forgotten? Did Dad mean so little to her? Or was it like she said—that she didn't know she needed to save them? That Dad would be gone?

All I have are the words left behind. Remnants of a relationship I hadn't known existed.

But what do the words prove? Or not prove? And do those words jeopardize the future now within my grasp? I don't know. Maybe—maybe not. But I can't take that chance.

I carry my father's phone into his bathroom and turn on the faucet. I fill the sink with water and hold the phone over it. When Fred arrives, I will tell him I found Dad's phone after the rain. Lying in the dirt. Ruined.

Of course, Idetta will know the truth. But she would never tell. I will explain—she will understand. She has to understand. Only what if she doesn't?

I bang my fist on the bathroom counter. Why am I suddenly unsure of the one person I'm sure of? Or is it myself I doubt?

My head swims with anger and confusion and the fear that my father wasn't who I believed him to be. Maybe I'm not who I believe I am either. Because even though Jenny said I am nothing like my father, the reflection in the mirror above the sink says otherwise. I have the crooked angle of his nose, the cleft in his chin, and his Basque hands with their thick fingers and wide palms. Hands made for holding on. Now all I have to do is get those hands to let go.

When the phone in my pocket rings, I jump—as if I've been caught.

I pull it out. Fred Big's name appears on the screen. I let it go to voicemail and turn back to the sink. Get ready to drop Dad's phone in the water.

My phone rings again.

"Damn it!" I click it on—"What Fred?"

His voice booms out—"There's been an accident."

> > > *driving the car*

The cat-piss smell of Idetta's Kia makes me nauseous. Or at least I tell myself that's the reason my intestines twist in upon themselves like the coils of a bull snake crushing a rabbit that only now realizes there's no escape.

When Fred told me there'd been an accident, I thought, *Idetta*. But then he said, "Jenny."

I didn't ask for details. Not even if she was all right.

"She's at Dr. Berria's," Fred said. "You need to come."

"Why do I need to come?"

"Because she's been asking."

"For me?"

"For Ferdinand."

The Kia's motor whines painfully as I push the speedometer to seventy.

I tried to call Idetta but got no answer. Probably left her phone in the truck while having Pascaline cut her hair.

An accident. Another accident. As if accidents suddenly sprout in Urepel like weeds after a hard rain.

I pull to a stop in front of Dr. Berria's office. Before I can uncurl my body from behind the Kia's steering wheel, Fred rushes over and blurts out, "It's all my fault."

"What are you talking about?"

"I kept pestering her—saying how she should move back to Urepel." Fred wipes sweat from his brow. "She kept telling me, 'I can't.' But I didn't listen. I tried again earlier today—she got upset and sped off in her car."

I put a hand on Fred's shoulder. "Sometimes accidents just happen."

137

"People say that." Fred rubs his right index finger across the sweat on his bottom lip. "But I investigate accidents all the time, and I'm telling you there's always something leading up to the fire or the crash or the fall—something that if changed, well...the truth is, every accident has a reason."

"What happened to Jenny wasn't your fault."

Fred rubs his hands together as if washing them. "Sometimes I just don't know when to stop."

My hand slides off Fred's shoulder. "Sometimes neither do I."

Before Fred can ask me what I mean, I pull open the door to Dr. Berria's office and step into the air-conditioned lobby.

The room smells of Lysol and lavender. Since it's Saturday, no receptionist sits behind the glass partition. I head through the door leading toward the examination rooms. Dr. Berria stands in the hallway, writing something on a notepad.

"How is she?" I ask.

"Broken left arm, cut on her forehead, some bruising."

"What happened?"

Dr. Berria shakes his head. "I asked her that, and she told me she got lost."

"Lost?"

"Yeah, on her way into town—on a road she's driven a thousand times." Dr. Berria glances at his notes. "Now how does something like that happen?"

"Can I see her?"

Dr. Berria opens the nearest exam room door. "She's sedated, so don't expect much."

Inside, Jenny lies on a table, eyes closed, head propped up on a pillow, a thin, white blanket tucked around her. The cast on her arm is still wet; the bruises on her cheek, still deepening.

Even with the cast and bruises, Jenny looks peaceful. No desperation distorting her features. No tears streaming down her face.

Back when we dated, Jenny would fall asleep in my truck while I drove her home. When we arrived, I would park and just sit there and watch her sleep. She always seemed so happy with her eyes closed.

Blood seeps between the stitches of the gash above her brow. I take a tissue from the side table where her phone sits and dab the blood away.

Her eyes momentarily flutter open. "Ferdinand?"

My voice shakes—"I'm here."

Jenny exhales. "They said something about you getting hurt."

"I'm fine."

"Good." A smile flickers across her lips. "Remember, you promised to take me dancing—I was worried you changed your mind."

"I didn't change my mind."

As Jenny drifts back to sleep, she whispers, "I didn't change mine either."

I pull my father's phone from my pocket. Beneath its dark screen lie texts written and sent. Words shared between my father and Jenny. Maybe the real reason Jenny deleted all Dad's texts was to make room for so many more. All the words of all the texts she expected Ferdinand to send her.

Dad dancing? I'd have liked to see that.

Before I turn to go, I set my father's phone on the table next to Jenny's—because the words his phone holds don't belong to me.

› › › *praying for light*

The wooden pews of Urepel's empty church are hard and unforgiving.

I tap my right foot against the floor, something I couldn't do until I was seven years old. Sitting in this very pew, my feet only grazing the tile if I stretched out my toes. After Mass, Louie, Jean, and I would get donuts. Chocolate filled with cream. The rush of sugar made us dizzy with energy and sent us running in circles until we collapsed panting on the grass. I haven't eaten a donut in years. The last time I did, the chocolate stuck to the roof of my mouth and the sugary cream turned my stomach.

As a boy, the pews offered me sanctuary from the summer's heat. No matter the temperature outside, the wood was always cool against my skin.

Is that why I'm here? For relief?

Only unlike the heat I left at the church door as a boy, I can't leave behind the ache of failure embedded in my bones. I will have to give Jenny half the insurance money—and so I won't have enough left to save the ranch.

I slide my fingers along the curve of the armrest. Maybe Jenny is still asleep—if I rush back, I can get Dad's phone before she wakes.

Too late for that you dumb Basque-O.

What will I tell Idetta?

Where will we go?

The back of the pew angles forward, jutting into my shoulders, as if trying to force me to kneel. I adjust my position—work to get the kink out of my neck. But it's no use.

Sunlight comes through stained-glass windows depicting the Stations of the Cross. Off to my right, Jesus falls to his knees under the weight of the cross he bears. On the opposite wall, he rises from the dead. Hands lifting toward heaven, light all around him. My mother liked that window best. She said, "The light is why we're here."

But what good is light if it illuminates nothing?

My head buzzes like the hum of an engine running without oil—*for my loved ones I would pass nights and days; nights and days, deserts and woods.*

My thoughts? Dad's?

"Uncomfortable as hell, aren't they?" The apaiza walks out from the vestry behind the altar. "People can only sit in these pews for so long before they start squirming. When I see that, I know to cut my homily to the chase."

"Dropping quotes?"

"Like hot potatoes." Father Kieran comes to stand in front of me; he grips the pew's smooth railing. "I would rip them out and have them replaced if the workmanship wasn't so beautiful."

"Aitatxi made them," I say. "I helped carve the details."

The apaiza gives me a wink. "The devil is in the details."

I hold my hands palms up. "No devils here."

"You still carve?"

"I used to love to—only now there's no time."

"There's always time enough for love."

I raise an eyebrow. "You, a saint, or a rock singer?"

"Bit of a mash-up." Father Kieran folds his hands together. "So what brings you to this uncomfortable church of mine, Xabier? Something you want to confess?"

My spine stiffens. "I have nothing to confess."

"I was kidding." Father Kieran grins. "Priest humor."

I let my body slump against the pew's back. "It's just... I don't know—you ever feel like you're being punished, Father?"

The apaiza comes around to sit beside me. "For what?"

"Mistakes you've made."

"Who of us isn't haunted by the ghosts of our failures?"

I sigh. "Any idea how to get rid of them?"

"I've found the best way to handle darkness-loving ghosts is to drag them into the light."

I turn to the window with Jesus rising. "The light is why we're here."

"Amen to that." Father Kieran bumps my arm. "One last quote?"

"Go for it."

"Rumi said, 'The wound is the place where the light enters you.'" Father Kieran lays a hand on my shoulder. "So don't be afraid, Xabier, to open your wounds and let in the light."

"Sounds painful."

Father Kieran smiles. "Exorcisms usually are."

"I'll keep that in mind."

"Uh oh." Father Kieran checks his watch and bolts to his feet. "The Irigoyen sisters invited me over for tea—and those two do *not* like it when I'm late."

I let out a whistle. "Talk about being haunted."

"I wish I knew a way to soften their...uh, demeanor."

"Ask them to make you a Picon."

"What's that?"

"Trust me, apaiza, a couple of those will take the sharp edges off the sisters' glares."

"If you say so." Father Kieran heads down the aisle. "See you at Mass tomorrow."

I wait for the click of the closing church door before I kneel.

› › › *walking the fence*

My forearms ache as I step to the next break in the fence.

My phone rings.

Idetta again.

Calling, calling, calling.

But me not answering—because I have no answers—about the past or future.

After leaving the church, I drove the Kia back to the ranch. Idetta was home by then. I wanted to go into the house, bury my face in my wife's lap, confess all the things I'd done and failed to do. But instead, I grabbed the hide-a-key from under the truck's front fender and drove toward the river where the foundation for the house Aitatxi and Amatxi never built sits like a brand on the land.

When I arrived, I climbed out of my truck and began stretching fence. Searching for the forgetful exhaustion hard work promised. My body moved instinctively, fingers sliding the wires into the stretcher, hands gripping, arms pumping, strands overlapping.

I fix and move on.

While I can't see the river from the fence line, its nearness makes the air heavy with moisture. Sweat stings my eyes and puddles at the base of my spine.

The burn of the sun spreads over the back of my neck.

If I were a different man, I would stop what I am doing, go home and tell Idetta about what is coming.

But I am more like my father than I ever knew and will keep my secrets as long as possible.

I go to the next break.

The wire here is thin, having been stretched before. Old breaks becoming new in the never-ending wheel of fixed and broken.

But when does something become too broken to fix?

I grab the strands, load them into the stretcher, and pump.

The snap of breaking wire is followed by the sting of a barb cutting into my face. Warm blood flows down my cheek. I drop the stretcher and press my hand to the cut. Blood leaks between my fingers.

I hustle over to the truck. Crammed under the back seat, I find one of the baby's blankets—blue cloth covered in winged unicorns. I press the blanket to the cut and check my reflection in the rearview mirror. The barbed wire missed my eye by less than an inch.

Dumb Basque-O—losing an eye won't fix anything.

I throw the stretcher onto the passenger seat. Then, keeping the blanket pressed to my cheek, I climb into the truck and drive along the fence toward the gate that opens onto the river.

When I was nine years old, my mother caught me on the riverbank searching for crawdads. Being at the river alone was something I was expressly forbidden to do.

"You want to be swept away and drown like Argia Mendixka," Mom said as she pulled me away from the rushing water.

Even though Argia disappeared years before I was born, the cautionary tale was repeated to each new generation of Urepel's children.

As a teenager, I learned that Argia's body was never found—and heard the rumor that maybe she didn't drown at all—she merely swam across the river to California to start a new life.

The fence takes a sharp turn to the left, which brings the river into full view—churned-up water, dark as fresh-tilled dirt. Dad always said when the river ran muddy it marked the sign of a coming storm.

But the sky is clear with no clouds on the horizon.

I pull the blanket away from the cut on my cheek. While the bleeding has stopped, a throbbing sends tremors of pain through my skull.

I whisper, "Uso zuria, errazu."

But the only thing left now to be told is the ending.

The gate looms ahead.

This near the water the creosote are thicker, so that the bushes grow up through the strands of the fence. Barbed wire cuts into the bushes and distorts their natural shape.

I put the truck in park and pull from my back pocket the life insurance policy my father took out on me. As I hold the folded paper in my hand, I remember the apaiza's words at Dad's funeral, "...your life is not your own; it has been bought with a price."

I set the policy on the passenger seat and step from the truck.

As I'm walking over to open the gate, I spot a familiar shape lodged within the creosote. A ewe has gotten tangled in the fence. Her body lies limp on the ground, a ring of blood around her neck.

It happens sometimes—the thing designed to protect, ending up killing. Though I'm not sure why. The fence is always there. The flock lives with it daily. Still, every now and then the sheep seem to forget how something known can turn deadly.

If I leave the body here, it will attract coyotes. With the lambs dropping, it would be like putting out a dinner sign.

Why do I even care?

I should let the coyotes take the whole damn flock. Only it's not easy to stop caring about something I've cared about for so long.

"Shit." I toss aside the blanket.

Flies buzz around the dead ewe. I swat them away as I crouch and push aside the sticky leaves of the creosote. Dull, dark eyes stare up at me. The ewe's pink tongue lolls out its open mouth.

"Dummy." I start to unwrap the barbed wire from around the its neck. "You couldn't see what was right in front of you?"

As if in answer, the dead ewe moves.

I stumble backward—"What the hell?"

The sheep's legs twitch—its hips convulse—and the top of a lamb's head emerges from between the ewe's legs. Another convulsion and the whole head pops out. The struggling lamb lets out a weak baaa, as if to say, *I could use a little help here, buddy.*

I scramble forward and work my hands around the lamb—grabbing onto its shoulders, turning its body. Blood spills onto the ground as I pull the lamb from its dead mother's womb.

The lamb greets the world with a determined baaa.

I retrieve the blue blanket from the truck and wrap up the lamb. Then as I cradle the lamb in my arms, a breeze rushes over the ground, mixing the pungent odors of creosote and blood with the musty smell of the river. A dust devil kicks to life and swirls around me. I close my eyes against the flying dirt as I listen to the beating of a heart. Not mine or the lamb's. But the pulsing heart of the land—beating, beating, beating—as its dream unfolds:

Mountains and valleys rise and fall.

Desert becomes forest return to desert.

Sunrise—sunset.

The moon waxes full only to wane away to nothing.

Days pass into years, turn into decades, stretch into centuries.

The land begins and ends and begins again—always changing, never stopping, racing into the unknown future as it calls to me, *Xabier, where do you think you're going? Your dream is here.*

I open my eyes as the dust devil falls away, leaving me dizzy, hands shaking. Overhead, the unblinking sun looks down on me, waiting for me to decide where the dream goes next.

With the bloody lamb nestled in my arms, I start to walk—away from the river and toward home.

When I reach the ranch house, Idetta again is sitting on the porch step, waiting for me.

Haugi and Txauri run over. The dogs bark and dance as if they've never seen a lamb before.

I open my mouth to tell Idetta what happened, but the only words I can get out are, "He lives."

I give the lamb to my wife, lurch up the porch stairs, and stumble into the house.

The baby sleeps.

Even though I'm covered in dirt and blood, I pause by his crib to breathe in the soft, sweet scent of talcum powder. My son's hands are curled into tiny fists as if he's ready for a fight.

"You can't fight the whole world." I find a clean spot on my shirt to wipe off my little finger. Then I work the finger into each of his fists, opening them up until his pink palms lie flat and exposed. "At least not alone."

I continue to the bathroom.

There, I clean the cut on my face—a thin, jagged line edged in blood. I crank on the shower. Steam rises in rolling clouds along the ceiling. I peel off my clothes and immerse myself in the water. The heat stings my skin, but I don't step out of the flow. I grab a washcloth and scrub my body until my skin turns pink and I feel clean in a way I haven't been since my father's death.

I dress and go downstairs.

On the porch steps, Idetta cradles the lamb on her lap. She feeds it with a baby's bottle.

I take a seat beside my wife. I don't say anything. She doesn't say anything. The hungry sucking of the lamb the only sound breaking the silence between us.

How did I get here? My throat raw with words left unsaid. My gut twisting with secrets. Idetta sitting right next to me but feeling miles away.

Idetta rocks the lamb in her arms as she looks at the cut on my face. "You're hurt."

I open my hands, palms sweaty, fingers tingling as blood flows into them. I reach over and touch the lamb on Idetta's lap. "There are things I need to tell you."

I start with the white dove and how I thought it was a sign from my father—hell, how I believed it was my father. Move to Jenny at the house the day of the funeral. "Ferdinand and I have been meeting up once a week for the last three months." My face flushes with heat. I keep going. In the field with Haugi searching for newborn lambs and Fred driving up. The foreclosure and the life insurance policy. "There won't be no investigation." How I didn't understand what he meant, not at first, anyway. *Suicide.* I tell her about using the come-along wench to raise the Farmall because I needed to prove what happened was an accident. And how the come-along broke and the tractor fell and the apaiza saw it all. "Understanding is like a shadow dancing on the wall." My mouth goes dry but I don't stop. I tell Idetta about Aitatxi and us talking and the fear of losing the ranch. "I can't wait for you anymore." I tell my wife about Jenny and my father texting—*I fear I have lost my arima*, and Jenny's accident and me giving her Dad's phone and losing the ranch. I end with the dust devil and the dream of the land and me not sure where that dream leads.

Idetta raises her right hand, and I prepare for the coming slap across my face. But instead of my face, Idetta slaps my leg. "You know you haven't rubbed up against me all week?"

"What?"

"Not when I was doing dishes or changing the baby or cooking dinner."

Of all the things I imagine my wife saying to me, this isn't anywhere on the list.

"Wait—you're mad at me for not being horny?"

"I'm mad at you for not being you." Idetta nestles the sleeping lamb into a blanket on the porch. "You might be a little lazy, Xabier, and very hardheaded, but you are also kind and open and honest."

"You forgot horny."

"That too." Idetta presses her palm to my cheek. "Oh, my Xabier, be the man I married."

"Why did you marry a dumb Basque-O like me anyway?"

"Because you wouldn't give up until I did." She bumps her shoulder against mine. "So don't give up now. Wherever the dream leads, we will go together."

I take her palm and kiss it. "My love."

"Now, about Jenny..."

"Nothing—"

—Idetta holds up her hand to silence me. "You loved her once."

"A long time ago."

"Nevertheless, there was something about her—your father loved it too."

"Why does that matter now?"

"Oh, my Xabier, what makes you think the thing you both loved in Jenny is gone?" Idetta strokes the sleeping lamb. "Maybe like you, she just needs to remember who she is."

"How am I going to get her to do that?"

"How should I know." Idetta folds her hands on her lap. "I've never met the girl."

I cringe. "Ooops."

Idetta smooths the front of her dress. "And as for your father, you forgot about the tripota."

"Tripota?"

"Your father loved tripota."

"I know, but—"

—"Xabier, your father was a practical man. He would not ask for tripota on Easter if he wasn't going to be here to eat it."

For a moment, I can't get my head around Idetta's words. My wannabe-ballerina wife's reasoning seems more than a little flimsy. Does she really believe my father wouldn't go to the trouble of preparing tripota if he didn't plan on being here to eat it? I doubt any court of law would see it that way.

But then I catch the sly smile on her face and realize it doesn't matter. What she said isn't for a court of law, it's for me. And for that, I love her.

I start to laugh. "He wouldn't."

"Of course he wouldn't," she says, as Louie drives his truck into the yard.

Louie leans out the driver's window. "Look who I caught trespassing on your land."

Jean climbs out of the passenger side and shrugs.

Idetta shakes her head and scoops up the lamb. "Go play with your friends."

Instinctively, Louie, Jean, and I go around to the back of the barn to drink beer. Only the barn no longer exists. The walls we schemed, laughed, and planned our lives behind are gone.

Jean kicks the charred ground. "No place to hide now."

"What do you need to hide from?" Louie uses a stick to flip over a blackened board.

"I just feel all exposed."

"You spend half your life in an open pasture," Louie says, "how much more exposed can you get?"

"That's work—this is play."

Louie shakes his head. "So were you working or playing out in Xabier's pasture?"

"I was just...well...you know..."—Jean drops his head as if searching the dirt for an answer.

"Helping me out." I squat and pick up a rock.

"You told me you didn't need help."

"That was before this." I wave my arm to encompass the missing barn.

Louie cracks open a beer. "Hell, insurance will cover the barn."

I stand up, take a deep breath. "I won't be making a claim."

Jean walks over to stand next to Louie. "Why not?"

"Because—" the words feel like they're covered in barbed wire; I force them out—"I made a pile of broken boards and lit them on fire."

Louie shades his eyes as if he can't see me clearly. "You burned down your barn?"

"No, or maybe...I don't know." I throw the rock I picked up into the center of what was the barn. "I was going to but then—"

—"Why would you do something dumb like that?"

I tilt my face toward the horizon where the washed-out blue of day darkens toward dusk and all I can think about is my father's last word hanging in the air and Jenny lying in the doctor's office and the bloody lamb cradled in my arms—and I want to take back what I said about the barn and just drink beer and talk about all the dumb shit Louie, Jean, and I did growing up. But when I lower my head and see the way my oldest friends are looking at me, I keep going.

"I wanted to hide what happened."

Louie squints at me. "The accident?"

"I'm not sure it was an accident." My voice comes out deep and throaty like at night, in the dark, when I tell Idetta things, secret things, private things that I would never speak of in the light of day.

"What are you saying?" Jean asks.

"The ranch is in foreclosure. Fred said I needed all the money from the life insurance to cover what we owed." I am breathing hard as if I've just run a long way and still have a long way to go and am not sure I have the strength to finish. "But I wouldn't get the money if what happened was...was...not an accident."

"What else would it be?"

"Suicide." Jean crushes his beer can beneath his boot.

"Huh?" Louie's face pinches. "I don't understand."

"I do." Jean uses the toe of one of his boots to dig a hole in the dirt. "Sometimes I feel like I'm caught in a steel trap—I'm not sure whether I should gnaw off my leg to escape or just give up."

"What the hell are you talking about?"

"I'm broke." Jean sighs. "Xabier gave me a job. That's what I was doing in the pasture."

"How come you didn't tell me?"

"I'm a Basque man who sucks at being a shepherd." Jean goes over to the twelve-pack of Coors sitting on the ground and grabs three more cans. "Not the kind of thing you like to brag about."

Louie takes a beer from Jean. "News flash, I'm a Basque man who doesn't eat lamb."

"Bullshit," Jean says. "I've seen you eat lamb."

"You've seen me push it around my plate but not how I slip it to the dogs under the table."

Jean whistles. "Anyone else know?"

"My wife—well, and the dogs." Louie turns to face me. "You told Idetta about your dad and the ranch, right?"

"Of course," I say as Jean hands me a beer. "Eventually..."

Louie pops open his beer. "Why'd you wait?"

I let out a slow breath. "I didn't want to admit how I messed up."

"Messed up."

"If I could just go back and change things..."

"Fuck that." Louie whips his arm through the air as if clearing away the ghost of the barn. "You said yourself you're not sure if it was an accident or not. And guess what, maybe your Dad wasn't sure either."

"What do you mean?"

"Maybe things were bad and maybe he wasn't thinking right and maybe he shouldn't have been trying to fix the tractor on his own. But the beam breaking at that exact moment, hell, no one could have seen that coming."

I'm not sure if what Louie says is true, but even so, his words make my breaths come easier.

Louie shifts his gaze back and forth between Jean and me. "Any other secrets you dumb Basque-O's want to share?"

"Dumb Basque-O's?"

"Yeah, secret dumb Basque-O's."

"Okay, here's some secret shit." Jean takes a long swig of beer, then blurts out. "Fred Big came over last night to talk about giving me a new loan."

"You want a bigger flock?" Louie asks.

"Hell no—I'm done with sheep." Jean raises his beer as if to

154

toast himself. "Cattle are my future. I'm going to be the best damn Basque cattleman in the world."

Silence hangs in the air as if Jean's new world is holding its breath in anticipation.

Finally, I ask, "What would your father say about you giving up on sheep?"

"Words in Euskara I wouldn't like to hear." Jean kicks the ground. "But damn it, it's my future and I'm going to be a cattleman."

At that Louie busts out laughing—"Best damn Basque cattleman in the world?"

Jean shoves Louie. "In the fucking world."

Which only makes Louie laugh harder—Coors shooting out his nose. Which gets Jean laughing. He shakes his can and sprays beer over Louie. Which makes me laugh. And just like that we are all laughing and spraying beer on each other and acting like dumb Basque-O's when Idetta steps onto the porch and calls out, "Time to go home boys."

Jean wipes beer from his eyes. "She sounds like your ama."

I punch him in the arm. "Get out of here you cattleman."

"Be back after dinner for night watch." Jean gallops over to Louie's truck like he's riding a bronc, climbs in, and yells, "Best damn Basque cattleman in the fucking world!"

Louie shakes his head. "What are we going do with him?"

"I guess help him become the best damn Basque cattleman in the fucking world."

"Sounds like a lot of work."

"At least he's got Fred behind him."

Louie gathers up the empty beer cans. "That a good thing?"

"Who knows."

"That must have been why Fred bought all that stuff at Mendia's yesterday." Louie sticks the empty cans into the Coors carton. "Some kind of symbolic coronation."

"Coronation?"

"For Jean's new life," Louie says as we walk toward his truck. "Bale of straw, some oil, and a rope I guess for lassoing steers."

"I'm surprised Fred didn't offer to go in halves with Jean," I say. "Take another shot at ranching."

"Maybe he will." Louie drops the Coors carton into the bed of the truck. "Just hasn't let Jean know yet."

I pick up a blackened oil can from the ground. "Another secret dumb Basque-O?"

Louie slaps me on the shoulder. "World's full of us."

As Louie and Jean drive off, I cock my arm to throw the oil can. But I stop when I notice the yellow beneath the soot. I brush the can off on my pants leg to reveal the remains of the label: *P*...*N*...*Z*.

Earlier, when I searched the barn for things to burn, I don't remember there being any Pennzoil cans. Only Shell. I bounce the Pennzoil can in my hand. Maybe I just missed them. It doesn't matter. I throw the oil can into the air, and as it clatters amid the burned-out remnants of the barn, I recall Fred's words, "Every accident has a reason."

> > > *when forever ends*

Before going to bed, I tell Aitatxi about the day.

Of course, Aitatxi doesn't respond. In the circle of light from the nightstand's lamp, his face is drawn and pale. His breathing so shallow the rise and fall of his chest beneath the rose-covered quilt is no longer discernible.

As I turn off the light, I repeat the words Amatxi sent me off to sleep with as a boy, "Ondo ibili ene maitasuna."

Maybe the words are what Aitatxi has been waiting for, because in the morning he is gone.

EASTER SUNDAY

...he is risen from the dead.

MATTHEW 28:7

When I step into Aitatxi's room, the bed is empty. The rose-covered quilt bunched against the footboard.

"Aitatxi?"

Did he just dissolve into the sheets?

I check the closet, drop to my knees and gaze under the bed. But my aitatxi is nowhere in the room.

A chair scrapes along the kitchen floor below me.

"Aitatxi?"

I race down the stairs, come flying into the kitchen—breathing hard, face flushed—to find Aitatxi sitting at the table eating a bowl of cereal.

"What are you doing?"

"I hungry." Aitatxi shoves another spoonful into his mouth. "I like the corn flakes."

I collapse into a chair across from him. My whole body goes limp because even though eating a bowl of cereal in the morning is something my aitatxi has done a thousand time, right now it feels like a miracle.

"Aitatxi...I thought...I thought..." For days I'd been watching him slip away. Dissolving before my eyes. As he became less and less a part of this world and more of the next. And even though this is what I've hoped for and dreamed about, I am wary. Because the Aitatxi in front of me now is not the Aitatxi from a week ago. That Aitatxi hefted a two-hundred-pound pig onto a steel hook. This Aitatxi's hand trembles with the effort of lifting a spoon to his mouth.

I reach across the table and touch his arm. "How do you feel, Aitatxi?"

He presses his lips together. "How many day it been?"

"A week."

Aitatxi nods as if calculating the lost time in his head. "That make this day Easter."

"Yes, it's Easter."

"We need a get ready for big Easter meal."

"Sure—I mean, we can," I say. "If you'd want to...it's just—Dad."

Aitatxi sets down his spoon. "My Ferdinand, he always like the Easter."

"He's gone, Aitatxi."

Aitatxi's patchy gray beard clings to sunken cheeks. "Ondo ibili ene maitasuna."

"You heard me?"

"That what Amatxi, she say a you every night before sleep—'travel well my love.'"

I put my hand atop his and echo his words, "Travel well my love."

Aitatxi nods and pushes his chair away from the table. "We need a hurry or late for Easter Mass."

When he tries to stand, Aitatxi wobbles. I rush to catch him before he falls and lower him back into his chair.

"How about I go to Mass and invite the apaiza to come see you after?"

"I think maybe that idea a good one."

"Idetta," I call. "Come quick—I found an Easter egg hidden in the kitchen."

When Mass ends, Idetta and I linger in the pew until the church empties and we can get the apaiza alone to tell him about Aitatxi.

"I'm so happy for you, Xabier." Father Kieran gives me a hug. "And you too, Idetta. I can only imagine how hard it's been for both of you."

Idetta bounces the baby. "That's over now."

"I will stop by the ranch to see your aitatxi once I get things cleaned up here."

"You will come to Easter dinner," Idetta says.

"I don't want to—"

—"That wasn't a question."

Father Kieran's face reddens. "Oh."

"Dinner at three," Idetta says as she adjusts the baby in her arms. "Drinks at two."

The apaiza smiles. "Picons?"

My face stretches into a grin. "Of course."

"Men." Idetta turns toward the door. "I'll wait outside while you two discuss the virtues of drinking."

As the door closes behind her, Father Kieran says, "Your wife sure doesn't waste words."

"She has a way of cutting to the chase."

"Maybe I should have her take a look at my sermons."

"Want to have all your quotes edited out?"

Father Kieran purses his lips together. "Hmm, baby steps on that."

"Thought so." Light pours through the stained-glass windows and falls over the empty pews whose waxed wood glows. "Besides, I could use a good quote right now. Got anything about why life is so damn confusing?"

The apaiza turns to the stained-glass window depicting Jesus ascending into heaven. "Kierkegaard said, 'Life can only be understood backwards; but it must be lived forwards.'"

"Well that sucks."

Father Kieran returns his gaze to me. "Then how about this: 'All you can do is laugh and grow strong.'"

"You?"

"Ignatius of Loyola." He gives me a slap on the back. "Give it a try."

"Sure, why not." I turn toward the door. "Remember, Picons at two."

The apaiza rubs his hands together. "I won't be late."

When I step outside, the glaring light of midday blinds me as my wife says, "She's not as pretty as Pascaline said."

I blink until my sight clears to reveal Jenny, her left arm in a cast, standing on the far side of the parking lot. "Oh shit."

"Did you break her arm?"

"What? No."

"Just checking."

Jenny uses her good arm to wave.

"Oh look, we're friends now." Idetta waves back. "You better go see what my new friend wants."

"You coming?"

"We're not that good of friends yet."

"Okay, then." I kiss the baby on top of his head. "Good times."

As I walk across the length of the parking lot to Jenny, gravel crunches beneath my boots.

Jenny looks past me. "Your wife's pretty."

"She said the same thing about you."

Jenny manages a slight chuckle. "Doubtful."

"Yeah, well." I dig the tip of my boot into the gravel. "Listen, about yesterday and what I said—"

—"Dr. Berria told me you stopped by."

"You were asleep."

Jenny scratches at the edge of her cast. "Why'd you come?"

My wife's eyes burn into the back of my neck. "Just wanted to make sure you were okay."

Jenny smiles wistfully. "Not sure I know what that means anymore."

"I'm glad you're all right, Jenny."

"Are you?"

Her response tightens my throat. "What are you going to do now?"

"Go back to Kingman, try and—"

—"I mean for Easter."

"Like dye eggs or something?"

I blurt out—"Come to the ranch for Easter dinner."

Jenny seems as confused by the offer as I am. She gazes at Idetta and the baby standing on the church steps. "I don't think your wife would like that."

"It was her idea." I turn and smile at Idetta.

"After everything... why would you want me there?"

I let out a long, slow breath. "My father wouldn't want you to be lost, Jenny."

Her eyes swell with tears. "I really cared for him, Xabier."

"I know," I say. "That's why I left you his phone."

"Phone?"

"On the nightstand when I visited you at Dr. Berria's."

Again, Jenny looks confused. "There was no phone, Xabier."

› › › *changing the past*

When I tell Idetta about inviting Jenny to Easter dinner, she frowns, then says, "Fine—she can help in the kitchen."

"I'm pretty sure she can't cook."

"Of course not."

I drive out of the church parking lot and instead of turning right in the direction of the ranch, I turn left.

"Where are you going?"

"I need to stop by Fred's."

Idetta turns to face me. "On Easter?"

"It's about the barn."

Which isn't a lie and not really the truth, but a kind of purgatory between the two—a place I've been spending a lot of time in lately.

"I need to get home and start cooking," Idetta says.

"Pascaline can drive you."

Idetta presses the tip of her tongue between her lips, thinking, measuring.

I force a smile. "She's coming out to help with Easter dinner anyway."

"Okay, Xabier, okay."

I pull into Mendia's Feed and Tackle and park by the front door.

Idetta lifts the baby from the back seat. "Since we're inviting everyone to Easter dinner, you might as well invite Fred too."

"I don't—"

—"If you can invite your old girlfriend, you can invite your father's old friend."

I slide the truck into gear. "I won't be long."

When I pull up to the curb in front of Fred's office, I don't turn off the engine. Not yet. I need to think about the reason I'm here—Dad's phone. If Dr. Berria found the phone I left for Jenny, he would've called me thinking I forgot it by accident. Which means someone else took the phone. And the only someone else that could be is Fred.

But why?

I contemplate just driving away and giving up on understanding. Leave this shadow dancing on the wall. Because there are some things I'm better off not understanding. Maybe I should just be thankful Fred took the phone and there won't be any investigation. Be grateful I still have the ranch and go home, kiss Idetta, and drink a glass of arno gorria with Aitatxi. Stop looking back and laugh and live forward.

I turn off the truck's engine.

The bell clanks as I enter Fred's office.

A strip of light comes from under the closed bathroom door. The picture of Fred and my father still sits on his desk. I pick it up. Focus my attention not on the image but the frame.

My fingers press into the tiny grooves etched along the border. A design carved in the wood. When I move the frame closer, the seemingly random lines take flight to become the wings of doves darting and swooping around the image of my father and Fred.

The toilet flushes. Water runs.

When Fred emerges from the bathroom, he doesn't seem surprised to find me waiting; he gestures toward the picture in my hand. "Ferdinand carved the frame."

My brow furrows with confusion. "Dad didn't carve."

"He stopped right before you were born."

"Why?"

"You," Fred says.

"Me?"

"Ferdinand took being a father very seriously." Fred takes the picture from my hand. "He decided to concentrate all his energy on his flock and taking care of his family. No time for things like carving frames for old friends."

"Is that what you two were—friends?"

"Let's just say we had a complicated relationship." Fred sets the picture on his desk and takes a seat. "I know why you're here, Xabier."

"Do you?"

He opens a drawer, pulls out my father's phone, and lays it next to the picture on his desk.

My heart beats stretch out. "Why did you take it?"

Fred's shoulders rise and fall with a drawn-out sigh. "Short answer or long?"

"Just tell me."

"A little for you—a little for me." Fred leans back in his chair. "But mostly for Ferdinand."

"You saw the texts?"

Fred nods.

"So you took the phone to save the ranch."

"This was never about saving the ranch, Xabier." Fred folds his hands atop his belly. "It was about saving Ferdinand."

"It's too late to save my father."

"You're so young." Fred shakes his head. "You'll learn—time passes and dreams slip like dirt through your fingers. In the end, it's not the dreams that really matter, but the life you make after they're gone."

"My father is dead."

"I'm not talking about his life—I'm talking about mine."

"I don't understand."

"Twenty years ago, I had the barrel of a shotgun in my mouth when Ferdinand knocked on my door." Fred curls the fingers of his hands—as if he can still feel the weight of the gun. "My wife and daughter gone. My life ruined. And the man I hadn't spoken to for over a year shows up and tells me, 'Don't let it end like this.'" Fred opens his hands and stretches out his fingers. "Ferdinand never told anyone. He gave me a chance for a future without...well, more of the past holding me down. I wanted to return the favor—that's why I offered to buy the ranch. But Ferdinand just kept saying, 'I can't.'"

"The ranch was his arima," I say. "He couldn't live without it."

"I failed your father in life—I won't fail him in death." Fred points to the picture of him and Dad. "Ferdinand deserves to be remembered for how he lived—not how he died."

In the picture, Dad is so young. My age. The whole world ahead of him. Anything possible. A whole life yet to be lived.

"My father's life was more than how he died."

"Of course it was." Fred puts his elbows on the desk. "But if Ferdinand hadn't knocked on my door that day, do you think people would have remembered me as anything but the stupid cattle rancher who blew his head off?"

Was Fred right? I trace the tip of my finger along the picture frame my father carved. Did the ending undo the beginning? Collapse the middle into nothingness?

I sigh. "You can't just erase the past."

"Sure you can." Fred smiles. "Just takes the flick of a match."

The barn burning—flames rising—Idetta running—my love, my love, my love.

I lunge across the desk and grab the collar of Fred's shirt. "My wife saw you in the barn—she almost died in that fire."

"I...I...I'm sorry—I didn't know."

I push Fred away. He collapses into his chair.

I step back as the world spins. What now? More lies—secrets—hidden truths? Was that my father's legacy to me? My future?

Something solid hits the office window behind me with a bang.

I turn. A white dove sits on the windowsill. Stunned. Black eyes fixed on me. Wings slowly opening and closing—as if unsure it will ever fly again.

I walk over and flip the latch on the window.

"What are you doing?" Fred rises from his chair. "I got the AC on—"

—I hold up my hand. "Be quiet."

I open the window, and when I do the one white dove becomes a hundred. The birds pour into the room. Filling the air. Wings grazing my arms, legs, hands, fingers. Touching my neck, cheeks, lips. I am surrounded by the beating wings of white doves—their cooing rising out of a hundred graves to become a hundred voices.

"Tell me," I say.

Amatxi—"Ondo ibili ene maitasuna."

Mom—"Your father wanted you to be special."

Dad—"Your mother would be proud of you, Xabier—I know I am."

Other voices mix with those I know. Separate—individual voices—all part of the same flock. Voices as old as stone. From the time before cruelty and deception took breath. Back when there existed only life and death and the bridge connecting the two. All the voices merge into one voice, uttering one word, "arima."

I blink and the doves disappear.

Fred still sits at his desk. "You okay?"

I place my right palm flat on my chest. One white dove remains; its fluttering wings settle into the beating of my heart.

"I can," I say.

Fred comes around to the front of his desk. "You can what?"

"I can sell you the ranch."

"Really? That's great." Fred slaps his hands together. "You can pay off the debt and have a little extra to start over. And I can save Ferdinand's good name."

I again look at the picture on the desk. "My father doesn't need saving."

"But Xabier—"

—"People need to know."

"They won't understand."

"Someone told me understanding is a shadow dancing on the

wall." I go over and close the window. "But what if we are the shadows? And understanding is the light that gives us shape?"

"What the hell you talking about, son?"

"I don't know what happened that day in the barn." I pick up Dad's phone off the desk. "Was it an accident? Or something else?" I stick the phone in my pocket. "I just know that trying to understand why and how my father died has changed me—shaped me into something new. Maybe it can do the same for others." I start toward the door. "Let that be my father's legacy. Now go ahead and draw up the papers for the sale of the ranch."

"Both parcels?"

I stop with my hand on the doorknob. "Both?"

"The original homestead, as well?"

"Aren't they connected?"

"Aitatxi owns those forty acres by the river outright."

Another secret.

"Just the papers for the main ranch," I say.

"Okay, but you know Aitatxi's piece is no good for sheep, right?"

"I'm done being a shepherd." I pull open the door. "Oh yeah, Idetta wanted me to tell you to come for Easter dinner."

"I can't—"

—"It wasn't a question."

Louie and Jean help me set up the tables for Easter dinner in front of the west pasture—where the breeze blows unbroken over the land and keeps away the flies.

When Aitatxi takes a seat at one of the tables, Louie presents him with a plate of the tripota he made from the pig Aitatxi and I slaughtered on Palm Sunday.

Aitatxi warily studies the blood sausage before taking a piece. He slowly chews. Louie leans forward anxiously awaiting the verdict. When Aitatxi frowns, Louie looks crestfallen. But then Aitatxi's frown turns into a smile, and he nods. "It good."

"Yes!" Louie claps his hands and grins like a schoolboy who just won first prize at the county fair.

Pascaline calls from the porch. "Louie, what are your sons doing?"

The answer is obvious—Carl and Max are chasing the chickens in circles and sending Haugi and Txauri into a barking frenzy.

"Coming." Louie rushes over.

Pascaline and Jean's wife, Maria, have been here for hours preparing the Easter meal with Idetta. Fred and Jenny showed up together about fifteen minutes ago. Idetta invited Jenny into the kitchen. Which makes me nervous—lots of sharp objects in there.

At least Dr. Berria is here in case anyone gets hurt. I found him in Aitatxi's room when I returned from Mass, stethoscope around his neck, shaking his head. "I guess Easter's as good a time as any to stop waiting."

Of course Idetta told him he was staying for Easter dinner.

Now, as I unload a box of arno gorria from the back of my

truck, I tell Jean, "Since Aitatxi has pretty much just risen from the dead, let's not let him drink too much wine."

Jean winks. "I'll cut it with water like he used to do to us."

As Jean puts bottles of wine on the tables, the apaiza pulls up. Before he even turns off the car's ignition, he asks, "Picons?"

"Idetta's making them in the kitchen."

Father Kieran rubs his hands together. "Excellent."

I pull open his car door. "Father, how would you like to have new pews for your church?"

"Comfortable?"

"Like sitting on a cloud."

"Don't overdo it." Father Kieran steps out of his car. "I can't give people even more of a reason to doze off during my sermons."

"Comfortable with a streak of attentiveness built in."

"Perfect." The apaiza places a hand on my shoulder. "So you've found time to get back to what you love."

"There's always time enough for love."

"And new dreams."

"Dreams come and go." I gaze over at Aitatxi. "And in the end, it's not the dreams that really matter, but the life you make after they're gone."

"Yours?"

"A friend of my father's," I say with a smile. "But I'm sure he wouldn't mind if you used it."

"I will." Father Kieran starts toward the house. "But right now, I need to go say hello to a Picon."

When the apaiza disappears into the kitchen, I turn and walk past Dr. Berria sitting with Aitatxi. The two of them are engrossed in an overlapping conversation in Euskara. Full of words I do not know but whose meanings I am beginning to understand.

On the far side of where the barn sat, I climb the slight rise in the land to gaze east at the previously obscured mountain—once blocked from view by what I thought was an immovable object that is now gone.

I imagine the Mamu on the distant mountaintop gazing back at me. My father with him. The two becoming one—always watching, always there. And I think about the day I chose to stay on the ranch and how my father became the center of a compass whose needle forever pointed home. When Dad died, the compass needle spun and spun, searching for a new direction—until I found it.

Idetta trudges up the slope with the baby in her arms. "You're going to have to drive the apaiza home, he's already on his second Picon."

I slide an arm around Idetta's waist. "How you and Jenny getting along?"

"She really can't cook."

"Told you."

"You tell me a lot of things—some more true than others."

"What if I tell you I'm going to build you a new house." I point west. "Right on the river."

Idetta eyes me suspiciously. "What have you been up to?"

I kiss her neck. "Tell you later when this dumb Basque-O has you alone in bed."

"Ha." Idetta hands me the baby. "I have to get dinner ready—take Ferdinand."

"Ferdinand?"

"You heard me." Then, before turning away, Idetta lays her palm against my cheek. "Oh, my Xabier."

I cradle my boy in my arms. "Oh, my Ferdinand."

As Idetta walks back to the ranch house, a thin layer of clouds moves in front of the sun—turning the shimmering orb soft and hazy. Muted light falls over the ranch's patchwork of green and brown stretching away toward the river.

Below me, the chickens cluck and the dogs bark and the sheep baaa. Aitatxi drinks watered-down wine with Fred, and Father Kieran and Dr. Berria sample the tripota; Louie roars past, chasing after his two giggling boys. On the porch, Jean and Maria silently kiss as Jenny and Pascaline step from the house, carrying trays of cheese and salami.

Only my father missing.

He told me, "Don't worry if you don't get it right, Xabier. You can always start over."

Now seems like as good a time as any to do that.

I hold Ferdinand close and feel the quick beat of his heart against my chest. I throw back my head and let out my irrintzina, "Ai-ai-ai-ai-ai-ai-ai-yaaaaa!"

The suddenness of my call startles the baby—he starts to cry—and in the rising wail of Ferdinand's voice, his first irrintzina entwines with mine.

In that ancient cry, I know him, and he knows me.

Glossary of English to Basque Terms

Basque language	Euskara
Basque Country	Euskal Herria
of Basque descent	Esqualuna
mother	ama
father	aita
grandfather	aitatxi
grandmother	amatxi
secret heart	isiliko behotza
white dove	uso zuria
priest	apaiza
blood sausage	tripota
Basque call	irrintzina
Basque Bigfoot-like creature	Mamu
my love	ene maitasuna
slang used to put children to bed	buba
Basque pastry	Gateau Basque
Basque cross	lauburu
red wine	arno gorria

About the Author

MARTIN ETCHART is a native Arizonan who received his BA and MFA in creative writing from Arizona State University before going on to get his PhD. His novels include *The Good Oak* and *The Last Shepherd,* which won an Independent Publisher Gold Medal for Adult Multicultural Fiction. He is currently a professor of English at Phoenix College, where he teaches creative writing and literature.

About the Author

Martin Dicolart is a native Arizonan who received his BA and MFA in creative writing from Arizona State University before going on to get his PhD. His novels include The Good Out and The Last Steamboat, which won an Independent Publisher Gold Medal for Adult Author rural fiction. He is currently a professor of English at Phoenix College, where he teaches creative writing and literature.